# THE
# UNDERDWELLING

## By TIM CURRAN

# 1

Second month on the job at the Hobart Mine in Iron City they put Boyd on the night shift and he knew he would be going underground where the raw ore was. No more sweeping up and running errands and driving truck, working the rock pile until his back was filled with needles. Maybe it meant he'd passed the initiation and maybe it just meant that they were short-handed. Either way, he was glad. Because this was what it was about: going down into the tunnels. It was cold and damp and weird down there from what he'd heard, but if you wanted to get in the Union, then this was the path.

And with a kid on the way, he wanted that real bad.

Russo, the mine captain, told him about it, getting right in his face as was Russo's way. The day before, as Boyd clocked out, Russo came right up, pressing him into a corner like he was horny and Boyd was available. "Hey, Boyd," he said, "how do you like this fucking pull? You figure on sticking with it or you just passing the time?"

Boyd told him the truth. "I'm staying. My old man worked the mines and so did his old man. I'm no different. It's in my blood."

Russo chewed on that for a few moments, nodding silently. He was a big guy with a crewcut and eyes black as coal chips. You didn't want to mouth off or give him any guff, but at the same time you had to stand your ground. Look him dead in the eye and let him know you had a set on you. He liked that. He didn't respect anything else.

"Now…you ain't gonna jump on me, are you? You ain't gonna get all girly and run off on me when things get tough and dirty below, are you? Not gonna cry your eyes out first time your pussy gets wet?"

"No, sir."

"Because I can't have that. I gotta quota to fill and if you bust me on it, swear to God I'll maroon your fucking ass down in the drift and it'll be the last time your little wifey sees your baby blues."

That's what the last month had been about.

When they took you on at Hobart, and they were real picky with all the damn unemployment, they put you through the acid test. They gave you every dirty, shitty, back-breaking job they could find. That's how they tested you and found out if you had the nuts for the job, had the mettle. Found out if you'd fold up on 'em or complain. Boyd did neither. They threw it at him and he caught it, never once dropped it.

Russo kept nodding, his breath smelling like salami. "Okay. Tomorrow night you're on the graveyard shift. Don't let me down."

And that's how it happened.

Boyd figured he was lucky. There were ten other guys hired with him but he was the only one they picked. Funny, almost like it was fate. Like what was coming next was meant to happen.

# 2

That first night on the skeleton crew, Boyd showed up twenty minutes early with his lunch bucket in hand. He parked his rusty Bonneville out in C lot, grabbed a smoke and looked up at all the buildings and huts dotting the rising hills above, the looming headframes and derricks and hoists that were lit up with blinking lights so low-flying planes wouldn't crash into them. Some of them went up five-, six-hundred feet, lattices of iron and steel that looked like the skeletons of dinosaurs against the night sky.

The stars were out and blinking and he wondered, somehow, if that was a sign.

But that was strictly bullshit, so he slipped into the Dry Room where the diggers changed out of street clothes and into working duds, showered up at the end of their shifts. Nobody was in there. Just Boyd facing those rows of battered green lockers and wooden benches, the cement floor stained pink from iron ore dust. It was hosed down every day, but ore dust is tenacious stuff. Boyd was aware of the silence in there, the dust hanging in the beams of the fluorescents overhead. On the day shift, the place was bustling, guys laughing and joking and swearing, talking football and hockey, tossing wet towels around.

But not at night.

The silence was thick and unnatural.

Like being in a morgue, a place where things did not move and voices did not sound, where only the ticking of a clock marked the passage of time. It all gave him the goddamn creeps. He wasn't one of these crazy jack hoo-hahs who believed in premonitions or any of that Mickey Mouse shit, but right then, he was getting bad vibes. Like currents of electricity were running from his balls right up into his chest. It made him feel funny inside, like something in there wanted to curl up and cover its head. He wondered if that was how people sometimes felt when they were certain disaster was looming. Refusing to get on planes because they got a bad feeling or how sailors and fishermen sometimes wouldn't get aboard a boat because they had the distinct feeling that she was cursed, that she was going straight to the bottom this trip.

No, Boyd wasn't a guy who got feelings like that, but he was feeling something. And whatever it was, it wasn't sitting on him too good. He had the craziest goddamn notion to turn around and run as fast as he could.

But he didn't, of course.

All he had to do was think of Linda at home, eight months into it, knowing that he was going to be a father and that straightened him right out. Feelings are just feelings, but families need to be fed.

The other miners started to pour in, swearing and smarting off at each other, and he relaxed. Just the jitters. It was going to be okay. That's what he kept telling himself.

The miners he knew said hi and the ones he didn't looked him up and down or ignored him completely. Boyd climbed into his gear and stood around with them, listening to them bitch and insult each other. Finally, a thin wiry guy with a face etched deep as pine bark came up.

"You Boyd?" he said.

"Yeah."

"Okay, you're with me, cookie. Name's Maki. This your first trip into the hole?"

"Yeah."

"Figures. I always get guys like you. Russo must think I'm some kind of fucking Boy Scout."

A couple of the miners laughed. They looked like they thought it was pretty goddamned funny that Maki got saddled with the Fucking New Guy. Boyd just stood there, not smiling or frowning. He was a FNG. At least for now.

Maki shook his head. "Well, I'll hope for the best, Boyd. I'll make a big wish that you don't get one of us killed."

"That's it, Maki," one of the other diggers said. "Wish with one hand and shit in the other, see which one fills up faster."

And then they were all laughing.

But not Boyd. Because what he was feeling was getting stronger.

# 3

---

Ten minutes later, the graveyard crew jumped on the trolley and made the run to the pit. "Trolley" was a pretty high-stepping word for an electric tram with ore-stained cars, but that's what they called it. The ride took maybe five minutes and out of the night came the pit. It was lit up like a football field for a Friday night game: an open pit some 300 acres across and over 900 feet deep, a huge cavern that had been sliced down layer by layer at Hobart for the past sixty years.

During the daytime, Boyd figured, if you flew over it in a plane it would have looked like some massive impact crater from a meteorite, except that it was cut square and even like the sides of a box. The whole thing was fenced in with a walkway encircling it, massive crane booms rising overhead that brought equipment down and hoppers of ore and crushed rock up to the surface. Everything, even the cranes and shacks perched on the edge, were lit up with spots and security lights.

The crew stood by the fence and looked down into the abyss.

A road snaked around its edges, circling slowly downward to the very bottom.

It was night above, but daytime far below. The pit was bright and busy and congested. There were buildings and warm-up shacks, great piles of slag and heavy equipment running back and forth. Lots of men scurrying about. It was like kicking over a rotting stump and exposing an ant colony, all that industrious motion and enterprise. While Iron City slept, the mines went on non-stop.

The crew rode an elevator down to the bottom of the pit. It was little more than a cage with fifty men packed asshole to elbow in it. If you didn't care for heights, you had no business on it. Boyd watched the lights as they descended. They were set into the rock face every thirty feet until the cage touched bottom. Then he climbed out with the others and Maki steered him around and made sure he didn't step into a hole. The entire way from the elevator platform to the rock face, he kept his hand on Boyd's shoulder. Good thing, too, because it was big down there, heaps of rock taller than two story houses scattered around. Shacks and trailers and the booms of cranes swinging overhead. Lots of big machinery—crawler loaders and rippers, scrapers and automated conveyors, 300-ton dump trucks that could have squashed you flat without feeling so much as a bump and immense electric mining shovels with buckets so big you could have parked six or eight full size pickups in them and still had room to walk around.

Maki brought them to a tunnel that had been shot through solid rock. Its mouth was vast; you could have driven a Greyhound bus through it. The rough-hewn ceiling overhead was set with incandescents like a subway tunnel. The lights continued on and on until they were lost in the haze, which was a pretty good indication of how far it went.

"This is the Main Level, cookie. That would be Level Number One," Maki said. "There are seven of 'em and an eighth they're cutting right now, some two hundred feet below Seven. With that one, this mine reaches down over 2500 feet. You'll want to remember that. It's a long way down. Any questions?"

"Yeah. Why you keep calling me 'cookie?'" Boyd said.

Maki turned and looked at him, shook his head, his face plunged in shadow from the brim of his miner's helmet. "You in the Union?"

"No."

"Didn't think so. *Cookie.*"

Boyd chuckled and Maki didn't seem to like that.

It wasn't part of the game.

See, they were playing a time-honored blue collar tradition called WHOSE GOT THE BIGGEST BALLS? It was Maki's game and he made the rules. He was the old hand, the working class sage, and Boyd was so green his nuts looked like limes. He didn't know shit. He didn't know enough to wipe his own bottom unless Maki handed him a rag and pointed out his asshole to him. That's why he had to tell Boyd how deep the shafts were, because a guy like him, shit, he was so dumb he'd fall down the first hole he found.

At least, that's how Maki saw it.

Thing was, Boyd had played the game before. He was thirty years old and he'd played it in the army and in lumber yards, on docks and in mills down in Milwaukee. No big deal. Maki was trying to make him feel uncomfortable, to assert his dominance on the working class food chain right off the get go. He was trying to intimidate Boyd, but it wasn't working.

And he didn't like that.

"You think something's funny, Boyd?"

"No, sir."

"Good. Let's keep it that way."

They came to a supply shack and were outfitted with rain gear and rubber boots, gas detectors and emergency breathing kits. Maki gave Boyd a quick overview of them, but you could see he didn't have much faith that a guy like Boyd would remember any of it.

They joined up with the rest of the graveyard crew at the elevator cage that led below. As they stood there, everybody grabbing a quick smoke before the big plunge, the insults and off-color jokes started flying like rice at a wedding. A guy named Breed started picking on Maki and Boyd was loving it. Breed was a big boy, looked like maybe he could crush rock with his bare hands. He had a black ponytail down his back and a bushy mustache, looked dark like he might have some Indian blood in him. He was always smiling and joking around. Boyd liked him right away. He didn't play the game; he just made fun of the guys who did.

Finally, Corey, the shift boss, called out names and checked them off on a clipboard. He was a heavy guy who looked pretty soft from sitting on his ass eight hours a day. But Boyd figured he was okay...as far as foremen went.

Corey came over and said, "You're Boyd?"

"Yeah."

"Good deal. We can use you. It's not so bad once you get the swing of it. You'll do all right. Maki'll show you the ropes."

"Yeah, just don't turn yer back on him or you won't be a virgin come morning," Breed said.

A bunch of the miners burst out laughing. Boyd wanted to, too, but he had to work with Maki. No sense pissing him off this early on.

Maki slapped his lunch bucket against his leg. "What's with you, Breed? Why you got to start that queer business all the time?

You like that kind of stuff? Is that it?"

Breed elbowed the guy next to him. "Hell no, Maki. I like girls fine. Just ask your wife."

"You better watch it," Maki warned him.

"No, Maki," he said, "I think Boyd there better watch it. We all saw the way you been looking at him. Callin' him 'Cookie' and all."

"Sure," said another guy. "You're his type, Boyd. A big vanilla cookie what he can take a bite out of."

They all burst out laughing, even Corey.

In fact, Corey laughed so hard he started to cough. It was just the typical working class ribbing. These guys always made with the gay stuff to see how thick your skin was. Maki couldn't take it, that's why they rode him. You work in a mine or a foundry or any blue collar situation, you had better be able to take it. Maki couldn't. He was thin-skinned and because of that, he went around with a target stuck to his back, spent his free time yanking arrows out of his spine. And once guys like these found your soft white underbelly, they'd never stop hitting you.

Maki, true to form, waded in like he was going to take a swing at Breed. Breed laughed. Corey got in-between them and told them to quit clowning around. Breed smiled, then blew Maki a kiss when Corey wasn't looking.

"Okay, that's enough," Corey said. "Jesus Christ, Maki, he's just riding you. Lighten up. That goes for both of you. Especially you, Breed, you fucking degenerate."

"I can't help it, Mr. Corey, sir. Maki just turns me on. Lookit that mouth on him, will ya? That mouth was made for loving."

"All right, Breed," Corey laughed.

"You better shut up," Maki said, his cheeks red as cherry tomatoes.

Breed laughed. "You gotta love his mouth," he said to the other miners. "He's got the whitest teeth I ever came across."

More laughter and jibes.

Maki, however, did not see the humor in any of it. "Do I have to put up with this? You better do something about him, Corey, or I will."

"Ooooo," said a couple of the men.

"You don't think I'm doing my job, Maki?" Corey said, his eyes hard. "Then you just go over my head. Go talk to Russo. You know how he feels for you. Call the Union or the Women's Defense League."

Boyd laughed with the rest this time. It was hard not to.

The cage came back up, bringing the diggers from the three-to-eleven shift. They were filthy from head to toe from another day working drift and scraping ore and cutting stope. They wore rain jackets and rubber boots, pants tucked into them. They were stained red with ore dust. Even their faces were pink. Only their eyes were white and a circle around their mouths where their gas masks had been. They coughed and spit out gobs of phlegm, joked with the night crew and made jibes about each other's wives and girlfriends.

Boyd and the others crowded into the cage and Corey locked it shut.

A siren sounded and down they went.

The cage moved slowly at first, but then it picked up speed, making a metallic whine that pierced Boyd's skull. His heart started to race and his lungs didn't seem to want to pull in air. In a rushing moment of panic, he thought maybe the cable had snapped and they were plunging to their deaths. Fifty men crammed in a cage would make one ugly splat 2500 feet down. But the cable was fine. The car rode down and down, sometimes smoothly and sometimes with unpleasant snaps and jerks, plunging straight down into the blackness. The only lights were from the car itself and Boyd watched the rock walls of the shaft speed by. The car dropped some men off at Level #2 and some at #4, #3 was abandoned, but most disembarked at #5.

They filed out and assembled over near the bell shack. Boyd noticed with unease the huge red cross on the wall, the stretchers stacked up like cordwood. Lots of safety signs were strung up with cute little sayings on them like, WATCH YOUR STEP, IT COULD BE YOUR LAST. There was an electronic display which listed the number of accidents this month. Only two, thus far.

Corey called out the assignments and the men grumbled.

Boyd stood there with his lunch bucket. Level #5 stretched out in both directions as far as the eye could see. There were tunnels snaking off it, airshafts punched into the ceiling and floor with hoses and lines running through them. The air was thick and damp and hard to breathe at first. Although Boyd had never been claustrophobic, he was very much aware of the mountain of rock overhead. Michigan was sitting right on top of them and anytime it decided to move, some of them wouldn't be coming back up.

All in all, it made his palms sweat and his heart race.

And that was Boyd's introduction to the underground.

# 4

Maki led him away through a serpentine maze of tunnels, this way, then that, and Boyd knew there was no way in hell he'd ever find his way out on his own. There were lights set into the tunnel ceiling every twenty feet or so, but they did little to cancel the gloom. It was just the two of them and everything echoed. Water dripped and shadows crawled, things scurried in the darkness and bats flew around. Maki didn't pay any of it any attention. They passed a massive hoist shaft and stopped at a ladder road, which was essentially a cribbed shaft with a ladder set into its face for climbing from the main level to the various sublevels. He went down first and Boyd followed. It was maybe twenty feet down. When they touched bottom, everything was so silent their voices echoed like rolling thunder.

The sublevel they were in was maybe big enough for three men to walk abreast, but no more. There was a set of little railroad tracks on the floor that, Maki explained, were used by the tram that hauled cars filled with ore to the main shafts where it was brought up to the pit. In the pit, the ore was loaded by those big mining shovels onto massive dump trucks for the ride up to the surface. The ore was then dumped only to be loaded again by mining shovels into railroad hopper cars that took it up to the refinery to be processed into taconite pellets. Its ultimate destination being ore freighters that took it through the Great Lakes to steel mills in Gary and Toledo, Cleveland and Buffalo, all points east.

"You got all that, cookie?" Maki said. "There's gonna be a test later."

"I got it."

"I knew you would, 'cause yer a bright fucking boy, ain't you?"

There were a couple loose cars on the tracks, red from ore dust like everything else. In the process of ferrying the ore down the tracks, lots of it spilled off to the sides. And that was Boyd's job. Cleaning up the spilled ore. It was no better and no worse than working the rockpile topside. He pushed the cars along and scrambled around on his hands and knees tossing chunks of ore into them. The whole while, of course, Maki leaned up against the wall or sat on a shelf of rock, bitching at him.

"Let's put some muscle into it, cookie," he'd say. "C'mon, use yer back, you fucking pussy. I ain't got all night."

He was a real sweetheart, that Maki, running Boyd down and telling him how lazy he was and how he wouldn't last, the whole time chewing on a sandwich and laughing. It didn't bother Boyd, though. He laughed right along with him and that pissed Maki off to no end. Once again, Boyd was showing no respect for the game and how it was played.

But Boyd didn't care about any of that nonsense, he was just glad to be busy, glad to be straining and sweating and getting dirty. It beat the hell out of standing around, feeling the rock above him and all those endless, snaking tunnels below. He couldn't shake that feeling he'd had in the Dry Room, like maybe this was the worst thing he'd ever, ever done. He was simply too aware of the dripping water and the creeping shadows, the darkness pushing in, the grim subterranean aura of the place.

It all reminded him about his old man.

He'd died when Boyd was fifteen years old over in the old Mary B. mine across town. They were cutting a drift and the passage caved in, crushing him and three others to death. Boyd's old man loved the mines. It was his thing. He'd worked at three or four different ones. And when he wasn't underground, that's all he talked about. When he was laid off, he worked in the woods, on commercial fishing boats, even sold cars, but all he thought about was getting back underground.

It was in his blood and that was that.

His own father, Boyd's grandfather, had worked this very mine back in the days of carbide lamps. He died when Boyd was six or seven. But the mines were all he talked about, too. Back then, they didn't use water and steam to cut down on the dust from the rock drills and they didn't have gas masks. The result being that Grandpappy Boyd was barrel-chested from silicosis and it was a great effort for him to breathe. He had to put his whole body into it to draw a single breath. He died in a hospital bed when he was eighty gasping for air like a trout on a riverbank. An ugly, awful way to die.

But Boyd didn't tell Maki about any of that. He was the old hand, the tough guy. And for the time being Boyd was okay with that. For the time being.

After about three hours, Maki called for a break.

They sat there staring at each other, chewing on pasties, the traditional Cornish meat-and-potato pies which had been brought over in the 19th century by miners from Cornwall, England and had become something of a local staple in Upper Michigan through the years. In the old days, the miners down in the shafts used to put their pasties on shovels and heat them with candles. But they were just as good cold.

Boyd was grimy and sore, but it didn't bother him a bit. The food tasted great and he felt very good, every muscle in his body perked up and randy.

"This the life for you, cookie?" Maki said. "No, I don't think so. You ain't got the balls or the brains for this line of work."

"If you say so."

"And I do. You won't make it."

Boyd looked him dead in the eye. "Sure, I will."

"You'll fold."

"You can't throw anything at me I can't take."

Maki didn't like that. He didn't like that at all. Because, see, he knew it was true. He knew damn well that Boyd was shaping up just fine and that bothered him to no end. Boyd was strong and he was a fast learner and he'd worked under guys like Maki plenty of times. In six months, Boyd would know more than he did and in a year Maki'd be asking him questions. And Maki knew it, too.

"Real tough guy, eh?" Maki said. "Well, that's good, tough guy, because I made you a date down on Eight, the new level. You'll be cutting drift down there, cleaning up after the charging crew. Dangerous work, cookie."

Boyd snapped the lid of his lunch bucket closed. "So, let's get to it and quit with the jawing already."

Maki liked that even less. He was half-way through his pasty and Boyd was stealing his break time from him. And not only that, Boyd was stealing his stage. He thought working drift would make Boyd piss yellow in his boots, but it wasn't working. Boyd wanted it.

"Well?" Boyd said. "Let's go."

Maki threw his half-eaten pasty in his bucket and called Boyd a mouthy little sonofabitch and then they were on their way up the ladder road, making for the main shaft. The whole way, Maki was doing everything in his seriously strained repertoire to intimidate Boyd and put the scare into him.

But it wasn't working.

Boyd was scared, all right. But not of Maki. Not of his stories.

It was something else and that something didn't have a name.

# 5

"You never know what's going to happen in a drift," Maki was saying. "Sometimes the charges misfire and they blow your arms off. Sometimes you tap into a pocket of gas and it's Goodnight, Irene. Sometimes there's cave-ins. Guys get squashed flat, cookie. I seen it once. A guy, friend of mine, crushed between two slabs of rock. All that came running out was something like red jelly. Those cave-ins happen all the time. Probably happen to you. Then I'll get stuck scraping your ass off the rocks."

"No, don't worry about it, Maki," Boyd said. "We'll be working together. If I go, you go. Won't that be a fucking scream?"

Maki was getting exasperated. "You think it's funny, cookie? You think cave-ins are funny?"

Boyd turned on him. Turned on him fast and made him back right up. "No, dumbass, I don't think cave-ins are funny," he said. "My old man died in one over to the Mary B. when I was fifteen. I don't remember laughing much."

Maki stood there with a dazed and helpless look on his face. He closed up like a flower and didn't have shit to say after that. His book of underground horror stories was plain used up. When they got to the cage for the ride down, he had a cramped, uncomfortable look to him like he was constipated.

Finally, he said, "Listen, Boyd. I was just letting you know that this is dangerous. I wasn't trying to be an asshole."

"Sure, you were," Boyd said.

Then the door was closed and the cage jerked and plummeted down into the depths of the earth, the air smelling of minerals and standing water.

When they stepped out, Boyd could taste the dust on his tongue. It was like the dust from a chalkboard, but grittier and thicker. He could feel it settle over his face right away and it made him want to breathe through his nose and sneeze a lot. There was a smell, too, one that he couldn't quite put his finger on…something like moldy rocks and crumbling masonry, a distinct and unsettling smell of antiquity.

"How do you like it here?" Maki said, looking down the carved tunnels where nothing moved but a pall of shadows.

"I like it just fine," Boyd told him.

But, good God, what a lie that was.

It was even worse down here than it had been on the other levels. It was like being in a tomb a mile underground and Boyd literally felt the walls closing in on him. This was Level #8 and the majority of it was still being excavated. He could hear the distant sound of hammers and machinery, but it sounded like it was coming from miles away. His heart thudded in his chest and the breath rasped in his lungs.

And he was getting that feeling again.

Just like before, that crawling, shivery sense that he was in grave danger. He'd written it off earlier as maybe simple paranoia couched with a healthy dose of claustrophobia given that his old man had been crushed to death years back at the old Mary B.

But this was something different. A separate species of dread.

As he stood there by Maki, next to the shaft house, feeling the great depths they had descended to, he had the weirdest sensation of déjà-vu like he had been through something like this before. Maybe not in real life, but perhaps in a dream. One of those cloying, crowded awful nightmares of suffocation that you wake gasping and sweating from at three in the morning. It was like that. As if he was slowly being asphyxiated by this place. It was a numb sort of horror, making him feel utterly helpless like a swimmer going down for the last time.

"You okay, cookie?" Maki said.

"Sure, I'm fine."

"You don't look fine."

Thing was, the smartass edge was missing from Maki's voice.

Boyd didn't believe for a moment that that prick Maki was actually concerned about his well-being, but he could sense a certain veiled apprehension under his words. Like maybe Maki didn't exactly care for it down there either. All Boyd knew for sure was that what he had been feeling was getting stronger. It was in his guts and crawling right up his spine.

*C'mon already*, he told himself. *Get a fucking grip.*

"You pussying out, cookie?" Maki said.

"Not me," Boyd told him. "You're looking a little green, though."

"Shit."

A few men in raincoats and miner's helmets came walking out of a passage. Two of them were just diggers, but the other guy was Jurgens, the mining engineer who pretty much ran the place. He was the guy who located the ore, instructed the men where to dig and where to tunnel.

"Hey, Maki," he said. "This Boyd?"

"Yeah. I got him under my wing, Mr. Jurgens. I'm showing him the ropes and all. I'm taking good care of him."

"Good. We can use the help. We're cutting a series of drifts down here," he said to Boyd as they walked off down the tunnel and the sound of machinery began to get louder. "There's no good quality ore where we're at now, so we need to tunnel to it. You ever done any drift work?"

"No."

"But he's a fast learner, Mr. Jurgens. You got my word on that. I'll teach him everything I know and make a first-class miner out of him. Yes sir."

"Good, good."

Christ, Boyd thought. Maki was kissing this guy's ass big time. Wasn't that just special? You had to love Maki.

They followed the tunnel for maybe fifteen minutes, turning off through a series of crosscuts, on and on. The whole way Maki kept trying to stroke Jurgens, doing everything but getting down on his knees for the guy. *How's your wife, Mr. Jurgens? Heard you went down to Mexico...was that nice, Mr. Jurgens? Is your daughter still in law school, Mr. Jurgens?* It was fucking sickening. Finally, they reached the stope, which was essentially a huge cavern cut by drilling and blasting. It was lit up by floodlights. It stank of sulfur and dankness. The ceiling was sloping and the walls set with jagged fault lines which Jurgens pointed out were from prehistoric volcanic eruptions.

"The rocks are different here," Boyd said.

"Of course, they're different," Maki said like he was some kind of idiot. "We're deeper."

"No, this is all limestone. Different from the shale above."

"That's right," Jurgens said, looking at Boyd like maybe he was wondering what a guy with a head on his shoulders was doing with a booger-picking moron like Maki. "It is limestone and I don't like limestone."

"Me neither," Maki said.

Jurgens ignored him. "And I don't like it because where there's limestone, there's water. Or there once was. That means subsidence, limestone caves. I don't like the idea of us blasting into one."

"No, that wouldn't be good," Maki said.

"See, Boyd, the ore is here, we just have to get through this goddamn limestone first." He led Boyd over to the wall and knocked on the striated rock there. "This is all limestone laid down during the Permian."

"Sure," Boyd said. "Sedimentary rock. Layers of mud and sediment."

Jurgens nodded. "That's right. Thing is, it just doesn't belong here. I mean, from a geologic standpoint, this is the first Permian rock ever found in Michigan. So that's something, but there's no goddamn ore in it. See, this part of Michigan is all old, very old Precambrian rock. Anywhere from 500 million to three or four billion years old. And this Permian strata is fairly new, roughly 250 million years old. It just doesn't belong here."

"There's no Permian rocks at all in Michigan?"

"None that I've ever heard of. No sediments or fossils. Erosion is partly to blame, but the real culprit was the Quaternary glaciation that raged right through the Pleistocene. The advance and retreat of the glaciers also stripped away eons of sediment. Just about anything after the Silurian is gone in Upper Michigan. So, obviously, this Permian strata does not belong."

"Then why is it here?"

"Some type of singularity, I should imagine."

"That's gotta be it," Maki said.

Boyd felt like slapping him. He had no idea what Jurgens was talking about and Boyd barely understood himself, but at least he was keeping his mouth shut. But Jurgens simply ignored Maki. Something, Boyd figured, that most people at the Hobart Mine learned to do very quickly. Jurgens went on, explaining that the Permian Period occurred at the tail end of the Paleozoic Era, right before the Mesozoic…which brought us all the dinosaurs and made guys like Steven Spielberg a lot of money. The Permian ended the Paleozoic with a mass extinction that wiped out like 90% of the life forms on the planet. It was a much more massive extinction than the one that wiped out the dinosaurs much later on. These Permian rocks were from that time period.

"We've got a guy here studying this strata, a paleobiologist from the U of M named McNair. He theorized that, perhaps at the time of the extinction itself, volcanic action or seismic activity caused this seam of Permian strata to be submerged, engulfed by the much older Precambrian shelves. Thus, preserving it here for us when the rest of the Permian strata was scraped and washed away long ago."

"So, it's a pretty significant find?"

"Oh yes. But there's no ore in it, Boyd, and they pay me to find ore."

On that note, Jurgens led them away through the stope.

It angled off to the left and things started to get very, very loud. Up ahead, the crews were cutting drift, some three separate tunnels through solid rock to reach the ore-bearing strata. It was quite an operation. There were tram tracks leading from the drifts to other tunnels, the cars coming and going, filled with rock that would end up topside in thepit. There were dozens of men moving around beneath the dead glare of arc lights and incandescents lining the walls. The smell of sulfur was eclipsed by diesel fumes and clouds of rock dust. Water dripped and ran in little streams. Engines hummed and rumbled. Air compressors hissed and generators whined. There were pipes and hoses and high voltage lines snaking all over the place. The thunder of jackhammers and pneumatic rock drills. Red mud splashing underfoot.

It was unbelievable.

Jurgens assigned them to a crew cutting drift far to the right. Maki and Boyd put on their gas masks and safety goggles, put in their ear plugs. It was a loud and dangerous place with the clouds of dust and chips of rock flying all over the place.

The drift was called a "dog drift" because it was barely large enough to work in. The drillers would sink a pattern of holes and then the charge crew would pack them with dynamite and everybody would get the hell out of there. The blast would clear maybe ten feet of tunnel and right away the diggers would rush in when the dust settled and go at it with picks and shovels, clearing away rock and debris. The only way to do it was to form a fireman's chain and pass the rock back out of the drift to the waiting tram cars. Even so, the dust was so thick you could barely see in there. Boyd knew there were men in there with him, but all he could see were the lights of their helmets bobbing in the murk. The claustrophobia he felt was a real, physical thing. They went at it nearly three hours, cutting the drift deeper into the rock a good twenty feet.

When break time came, they retreated far back into the stope where things were a bit quieter. Boyd's boots were thick with red mud and he was stained head to toe with ore pigment, covered in a good half-inch of pulverized rock dust. When he took off his helmet and mask, it was in his hair. It was down his back and up his sleeves. He could taste it on his tongue. It was nasty stuff.

Maki and he sat around with a couple miners named Izzy and Johnson who didn't say much. Boyd was glad when Breed came over. Maki wasn't happy to see him, of course.

He poured Boyd a cup of coffee from his Thermos and Boyd washed the dust from his mouth. "Thanks," he said.

"You still a virgin, kid?"

"So far."

"What do you think of working drift?"

Boyd pulled on his cigarette, holding it with pink, greasy fingers. "Compared to what?"

"Yeah, that's how I feel about it, too. Not so bad, though. It's going fast. Jurgens said we should be hitting ore by tomorrow afternoon at this rate."

"Jurgens don't know his ass from a fucking stump hole," Maki said.

"You hear that, Boyd?" Breed said. "Our boss don't know shit. Too bad we couldn't have Maki here running the show."

"Oh, shut up," Maki said.

"Jurgens ain't so bad," Breed said.

"No, he seems okay," Boyd said.

Maki grunted. "You two were chatting it up like a couple old ladies at a Christmas fucking tea."

"He was telling me about the rocks."

"Yeah, he likes to talk about rocks," Breed said, stubbing out his cigarette. "You got to meet this paleo guy from the University. McNair. He really likes rocks. We dug out this fossil the other day…some kind of fish with teeth like roofing nails. McNair got so excited I thought he was going to cornhole the damn thing."

"How long you been at this?" Boyd asked him.

Breed laughed. He was always laughing. "Fifteen years, give or take. I'm just biding my time until I can get out."

"Sure," Maki said. "Breed's a fucking injun. He's waiting to get some of that free Indian casino money so he can be as lazy and useless as the rest of the tribe."

"Don't be making fun of my red brothers," Breed told him. "He's right, though, Boyd. I'm waiting to get on the list. Free money. Then I'll spend my days laughing at you white men and putting the dick to your wives while you're pulling your shift in the hole."

Boyd laughed.

Maki grumbled.

One of the other miners said, "You're a piece of shit, Breed. You know that?"

"My old man told me that from day one, brother. But way I look at it, if you're good at something, you go with it."

Boyd listened as they bullshitted around about the rocks and all the marine fossils they were finding that McNair said were laid down from an ancient seabed. Of course, Breed found ample opportunity to insult Maki and make jokes about his wife's privates.

Then Corey showed. "All right, you lazy sonsobitches, back at it! Chop! Chop!"

Breed offered him a big smile with his dirty face. "Hey, Corey? I ever tell you how much I love you?"

"Not as often as your wife does."

# 6

On it went.

    The work was hard, positively grueling. The charge crew would blast and then the diggers would clean the shaft out, haul out the big rocks and start shoring the tunnel up with braces and timbers so it wouldn't fall in. Boyd was glad for the work, glad to be doing something other than letting his imagination run wild. Because it was real easy to imagine things in the drift where you couldn't see five feet in the clouds of dust and drifting sediment, the ceiling pressing down on you and the walls closing in.

He could just about imagine what it would be like to be trapped by a cave-in.

If you weren't crushed, you'd be sealed in a sarcophagus of rock, slowly going mad as the air ran out and your helmet light dimmed, dimmed, and then went out for good, trapping you in that thick, godawful blackness. It was no wonder his guts were crawling.

But the hard work helped. Busting your ass in there, you didn't have time to worry about bullshit like that and from where Boyd was sitting, that was a good thing.

The boys kept blasting and the crew kept digging and then on around five a.m. the shit hit the fan.

The charging team blew their dynamite and Maki and Boyd were the first ones into the drift. The rocks were big, so they went in with jackhammers and chopped them down to a manageable size. Ten minutes into it, Maki stopped.

He pulled off his gas mask and Boyd followed suit.

"What is it?"

Maki kept shaking his head. "Smells funny, don't it?"

And he was right: it did. "Yeah," Boyd said, something in his stomach not just crawling now, but flopping around. "Like age. Like something real old."

He likened it to the stench you'd smell upon digging your way into a crypt. The odor was weird and dry, a stench of spices and time and stillborn air. Just a hint of it, but enough to make you gag. It was there and then it was gone.

The gas detectors weren't picking up anything, though.

Somebody down the drift yelled, "Hey, you two wanna quit sucking tongue and get to work?"

Boyd laughed and pulled his mask back on. Maki did the same.

The dust was thick in the air and Boyd couldn't see much. Just the blazing light of Maki's helmet, some dirty illumination thrown against the contours of his face. But he was willing to bet that he was scared. He'd heard it in his voice and you can't disguise something like that. Boyd was feeling it, too, but then he'd been feeling it all night, a strange and inexplicable apprehension like something was circling him in the dark, preparing to slip up behind him and take a meaty bite out of his ass.

Nerves. That's what.

They got back at it, using the jackhammers to break up the boulders that were too big to carry out. It kicked up a lot of dust and debris and little sharp-edged bits of stone that would cut you like razor blades if they had the proper velocity behind them. After a good fifteen or twenty minutes of that, they ditched the jackhammers and the crew formed another daisy chain, passing the rocks out, clearing the drift sufficiently so that it could be properly shored up. It was backbreaking, monotonous work, but they kept at it.

Maki was right in front of Boyd…and then he wasn't.

Boyd saw him lean over and grab a big rock and then the ground shifted and he simply disappeared. At first Boyd thought maybe a cloud of dust had enveloped him. But then he saw a big black hole leading straight down and Maki clinging to the lip of it with his fingertips.

He stripped his mask off. "Shit! Oh, shit! Hey! Back here! We got trouble!"

What surprised him most was that he did not panic.

Not really.

Something like that should have been second nature. But there was simply no time. He went down on his knees and sidled up by the hole, waving dust away. Poor Maki was hanging on for dear life. His mask had nearly come off, hanging by one strap. And his voice, God, it was loud and shrill and cracking: *"Boyd! Boyd, get me the fuck outta here! Don't let me fall! Oh please Christ in heaven…don't… let…me…fall…"*

Boyd had no intention of that.

The only thing that stopped him as he reached for Maki was that it was not over with.

There was a rumbling sound from below.

Then a hollow, groaning noise came up from the subterranean depths like wind blown through a pipe. There was a moment of suction that accompanied it and Boyd was nearly sucked down like a breeze through a smoke hole. He heard a booming sound from far below and knew it was caused by an instantaneous and abrupt shift in air pressure. Kind of like a sonic boom when air collapses back into the void left by a supersonic aircraft. Something like that. The atmosphere of the mine itself suddenly filling a great, empty vacuum down there. *Boom.*

All of that lasted only a second or two and the sucking was replaced by a sudden rushing of black, stagnant air that blew right into his face with gale force like something at the bottom of that stygian hole was exhaling. It hit him, made him teeter uneasily, an awful, dry smell about it. He'd never smelled anything quite like it before: just the raw, hoary breath of incredible antiquity.

"Boyd…"

He reached down and snagged Maki by the collar, pulling hard as he could, but right away, his knees started skidding towards the mouth of the hole from Maki's combined weight and the fact that he was struggling. Boyd realized with a sudden gush of fear in his belly that he was going over the edge, too. But he refused to let go. Then Breed showed. With the incredible strength and impeccable balance that comes with mining for a living, he took hold of Maki and yanked him up and out. And Boyd with him. Yanked them both up and out with those massive hands of his.

Maki fell right on top of Boyd like he wanted to roll him over in the clover, gasping and crying and spitting. Boyd pushed him off, but Maki wouldn't let go. He grabbed and held on.

"You saved my fucking life, Boyd," he said, his eyes huge and white in that dirty face of his. "Oh, by Jesus, you saved my life."

"Hell, I did. It was Breed. He saved both our asses."

Breed chuckled. "Goddamn idiots. I turn my back for one minute and you both fall in a pissing hole."

By then Jurgens was there with a big flashlight. "What in the hell happened?" he said.

Boyd took in a breath, let it out slow. "Maki picked up a rock and the ground just fell away."

"Yeah, I picked up a rock and the ground fell away," Maki reiterated for clarity. "That's what happened. If Boyd hadn't of grabbed me…"

Jurgens was near the edge with his flashlight, shining it around down there. The dust was so thick in the beam it looked like smoke from a bonfire, clotted with specks of swirling dust and debris.

"That's a funny looking hole," Breed said.

And it was. As Jurgens played the light around, they all could see what Boyd already had: that it was nearly circular, smooth and glossy like it had been burned through the rock and not dug with tools. It almost looked like the inside of a foundry smokestack.

"Looks artificial," Maki said.

Boyd looked at him. "Way down here?"

"It's not artificial," Jurgens explained. "Glacial meltwater tunneled it out thousands of years ago. The water constantly funneling through it smoothed it out."

Lots of miners had crowded into the drift and were muttering about the hole. All work had ceased back in the stope. The generators and compressors were still running, but that was about it.

"Let's find out how deep it is," Jurgens said.

Since there was no high tech echo-sounding equipment handy, he called out for 500 hundred feet of rope. When it got there five minutes later, Jurgens got out his tape measure and marked off the rope every ten feet with a black magic marker. Then he began to lower it down there with a stone tied to the end for weight. Nobody said a word as he did so. 420 feet of rope went down before it hit bottom.

"Pretty damn deep," Breed said. "You'd have been nothing but one ugly shitsplat at the bottom, Maki."

"All right," Jurgens said. "Clear this drift, you men. I want it cleaned out and shored up. And call up to Russo. I want a winch and a basket down here."

"What for?" Maki said.

"Because somebody's going down there."

# 7

Right away, Maki jumped on that one, rode it for all it was worth. "Well, it ain't gonna be me," he said as they cleared out the drift. "It ain't gonna fucking be me. Every time some shit job shows up, goddamn Jurgens calls for me. Like I got the biggest shovel and I don't mind the smell. Well, believe you me, Boyd, I ain't going down there. No way in hell am I going down there."

"So, don't," Boyd told him. "He can't make you."

"Damn straight he can't. I'd like to see him try. I'd be all over him. He doesn't want to get me going, no sir. I'd jump his shit and stomp it flat. It would take three cops to get me off him. You can take that to the bank. Hell, yes."

"Take it easy," Boyd said.

"I ain't taking it easy. I know how that guy works. He's always had it in for me. But not this time, not this time. He tries and I'll call the Union. I'll shove a dozen grievances right up his ass sideways, that's what."

Jurgens came walking up. "C'mon, boys, we got work to do here. Let's go."

And Maki, true to form, almost knocked Boyd down getting to it. "I'll take care of it, Mr. Jurgens."

Boyd shook his head.

They hit it pretty hard. In about two hours they had the drift widened to accommodate a portable winch that was pushed in there on lengths of track. Once the ceiling was braced up, there was nothing to do but wait and see what Jurgens decided next.

Jurgens was gone for about twenty minutes, but when he returned he had McNair, the paleobiologist, with him. McNair was a short, round little guy with a shaggy gray beard. He looked more like a prospector than a scientist, but he would do in a pinch.

"Okay," Jurgens said. "Dr. McNair and I are going down. I'd like a couple volunteers to go with us."

Not a man moved. Maybe they didn't like that aged odor

whispering up from the shaft and maybe it was something else, the idea that whatever was down there had not been disturbed in a very long time. Like the depths of an Egyptian tomb with a curse on it.

"I'll go," Boyd said.

"Me, too," Breed chimed in.

"Good, good," Jurgens said. "Probably nothing down there, but we need to have a look. We got caves or subsidence, we might have to cancel this drift altogether."

Maki looked from Boyd to Breed again and again. Then over at Jurgens. There was something brewing in him. He was ancy and wide-eyed. "I'm going, too," he said.

"I don't need you," Jurgens told him flat out.

"I got seniority over Breed and Boyd," Maki said. "If anybody goes down, it should be me. I'm the most experienced."

One of the miners giggled at that.

"I am. I been here longer than most. I got the seniority."

Jurgens said, "This isn't a matter of seniority, Maki."

"I'm going. I'm the one that should go."

Boyd laughed. "An hour ago, you were bitching that you didn't want to go."

"I never said any such thing."

Jurgens sighed. "All right, Maki. You can go." He just caved-in, knowing that if he didn't allow it Maki would whine and stomp his feet and make a general nuisance of himself like a spoiled brat until he got his way. And that would burn precious time.

Once the basket was hooked up to the winch, Jurgens and McNair went down. They took a walkie-talkie with them and called up that it was okay for the others to descend.

"You sure you want this?" Boyd said to Maki.

"Yeah, they'll need me."

Which was silly. Did anybody really need Maki? The only reason he was going was because he was still playing the big balls game, trying to show Boyd what a tough customer he was. It was silly. Absolutely silly.

They all wore rubber boots, helmets, and raingear. They took flashlights and gas masks. McNair and Jurgens had taken cameras, gas detectors, and Coleman battery lanterns down with them. It was a long ride down through that cloying darkness, the basket bumping around in the narrow shaft.

About half way down, Breed said, "Hey, Maki? Your mother have any kids that lived?"

And down they went into the underworld.

# 8

———————————————————————————————————

When they touched bottom, Boyd was glad to see the lights from the lanterns. They lit up the gloom enough so that he could see right away that this was going to be no quick excursion: there was a tunnel down there leading off into the earth.

"Limestone cave," Jurgens said. "Just like I thought."

That meant trouble for future mining operations and he didn't like it. McNair, on the other hand, was clearly excited.

"You boys ready for a hike?" he said, snapping a few photographs with a flash.

Jurgens and McNair led from the front and the others followed behind down a long, low-ceilinged passage that seemed to wind all over the place, the roof sloping so low at times they had to duck down. The gas detectors told them the air was fine, but they kept their masks handy. You just never knew. Their lights bobbed and splashed illumination onto cold, black rock that had known nothing but darkness for God only knew how long. It was chilly and damp down there and they splashed through puddles, feeling less like miners and more like cave explorers. Now and again, McNair and Jurgens would pause and study the strata.

"We're still in that Permian seam," McNair said.

Jurgens looked at him. "Way down here?"

"Oh yes."

Boyd was bothered by that and he wasn't sure why.

*So, these are Permian rocks…what of it?* he told himself. *You tripped over 'em on the surface you wouldn't have known if they were Permian or Triassic or Devonian for that matter. Rocks are fucking rocks.*

And that sounded good, sounded reasonable, but it wasn't buying beans. Because he was getting that feeling low in his belly again like something had curled up and gone to sleep, and now it was waking up.

His knowledge of geology was mainly from a high school class where they had grown crystals and collected fossil seashells. That was the extent of it. Yet, the idea of the Permian rocks was eating away at him. Maybe it was the atmosphere of the place...the age, the silence broken only by dripping water, that smell of entombed things only now bursting free. It made no sense. Regardless, he felt claustrophobic again, manically so. Like he had been buried alive.

Breed and Maki weren't saying much.

No bickering, no whining from Maki, and no insults from Breed. Boyd figured that was a pretty good barometer. It told him that they were feeling the forbidding atmosphere of this place same as him.

McNair and Jurgens led them into what looked like a stope that had been chiseled from the limestone, but Jurgens said it was probably hollowed by subterranean waters long, long ago. Just how long he did not even begin to speculate. And you could plainly hear the disappointment in his voice. A network of underground caves was bad news. It meant maybe abandoning the series of drifts above and channeling in a different direction. Things the company would not like because that meant time and money. Things Jurgens was supposed to be saving them whenever possible.

The stope went on for maybe another fifty or sixty feet, the floor littered with debris and collapsed shelves of rock that had fallen in long ago. Some were so big they had to climb right over the top of them. But they pushed on, the lanterns creating jumping shadows that crept along the crumbling walls.

Then it opened up into a massive cavern.

Boyd whistled at the sight of it.

"Holy shit," Maki said.

It was incredible. They stood there in awe, feeling like the first men to set eyes on the Carlsbad Caverns. Before them was an immense grotto. Even with the long-barreled flashlights, they could barely see the roof above. It had to have been well over a hundred feet straight up. There were huge stalactites and stalagmites, great shelves of rock that had been sculpted and polished by eons of dripping water into great columns and blobby, candleflow heaps of stone. Minerals sparkled in the walls. Crystal formations rose like pillars of salt. Great boulders the size of two-story houses had been perfectly rounded by ancient waters. There was a briny stink in the air.

"Gentlemen," McNair said, "we are about to step into the history books."

Maki stood there with his mouth hanging open as the flashlights scanned about, their beams thick with suspended dust and droplets of moisture. He swallowed, licking his lips. "Did somebody dig this out?" he said.

"No, no, this is a natural cavern," McNair was quick to point out before imaginations started running wild. "All of what we've seen so far has been channeled out of the limestone by ancient floodwaters. This cavern, too. It's really incredible."

"But that shaft I almost fell down…it was so smooth and round."

"That could have been volcanic rock laid down by a lava flow," Jurgens pointed out. "Lava can form shapes that look man-made if it rapidly cools."

McNair nodded. "Exactly. It'll take years and years of study, gentlemen, to answer all this. For now, just enjoy."

Thing was, all this might have gotten a paleobiologist excited, but Boyd and the others had mixed emotions. Something this big and this old, well it inspired a certain superstitious dread that made their mouths go dry. They were afraid of it and, at the same time, desperately curious.

"What're you thinking?" Boyd said to Breed.

The dazed look in his eyes finally faded. He laughed. "I was thinking of those comic books I read when I was a kid. Those guys in there were always finding places like this and they were always full of dinosaurs and shit."

It was McNair's turn to laugh. "I don't think we'll find any dinosaurs."

"Good," Breed said. "Because I left my rifle in the truck."

They all got a little chuckle out of that.

The floor of the cavern was about twenty feet down from the opening of the stope. But it was a gradual incline littered with rocks and boulders and there was no trouble climbing down. Jurgens and McNair went first. Boyd and Breed followed. But Maki waited above.

They put their lights on him.

"C'mon, peaches," Breed said. "I'll hold your hand."

But Maki was not moving.

"You don't have to come with us, Maki," Jurgens said. "All of this, it's above and beyond. I can't even say how safe it is."

"I'll stay with you if you want," Boyd told him.

That got Maki down. He was looking pale and his lower lip kept jumping with a tic. He was scared and nobody made fun of that, not even Breed. Maybe they were all feeling what Boyd had been feeling all night: the sense of impending doom. Like a can of something crawly had been opened up in their guts.

The floor was irregular, sometimes smooth and flat, other times hilly with mounds of rocks and jutting spokes of limestone. There were pools of water and lots of cracks that led down far below. Jurgens and McNair were having themselves a good old time, theorizing about the age of the cavern and the waters that must have cut it out, chipping off rock specimens and prodding at fossils…of which, there were many corals and brachiopods and crinoids.

"This is definitely late Permian," McNair said as he took photographs of the fossiliferous rock. "The index fossils are fairly conclusive. My God, look at these specimens. Trilobites and mollusks and ammonites. Enough to fill a dozen specimen cases."

"Sure, great scientific stuff," Jurgens said. "But my bosses won't be thrilled. I can tell you that much. If we have to divert those drifts, it'll cost thousands, hundreds of thousands."

"They'll live," Boyd said to him. "Besides, I bet museums will pay plenty for the stuff down here. *Christ*, people'll want to tour this. This will be a cash cow for Hobart. They'll rake it in."

"Yeah, he's right," Breed said.

Jurgens and McNair kept taking samples, discussing matters geological and paleontological, taking pictures. Boyd and the others wanted to explore, to see what was ahead. But it was hard to get them to move on. They wanted to study what they were finding. Finally, Breed and Maki moved off. Boyd went with them.

"Hey, we got bones over here," Breed called.

That got them moving.

Jurgens and McNair came right over, holding their lanterns out. There *were* bones. Hundreds–maybe thousands. Some were protruding from the floor and others thrusting out from shelves of rock. All of them were fossilized, of course.

"Amazing," McNair said, photographing them. "Absolutely amazing." He held his lantern over the fossil imprint of a fish that was sinuous and eel-like. "Ancanthodian. Last remaining forms died out in the Permian Extinction event." He looked around at the fossiliferous deposits. "Permian fishes...reptiles...amphibians. All heaped together like this. It's unusual. I suppose the waters must have brought them together."

"What's unusual about it?" Boyd asked.

"Well, some of these are land forms and others are marine animals. It's hard to imagine what could have scattered them all into the same basin. I suppose it could have been a streambed. Animals have a habit of dying around streams and in the shallows. The water might have washed them here."

Boyd looked at all those knobs of bone and things like the slats of ribcages, jaws, and skulls, and you name it. The bones of animals from land and from the sea all tossed into this basin like McNair said. No, it didn't make sense. Not even to a guy like him. If there were a pile of bones like this in the modern world, he would have thought somebody collected them up and put them there. Or dumped them there.

*Sure*, he thought, *like the litter pile of bones outside the cave of a beast. When something was done eating, it just tossed them in a litter pile.*

But he didn't say that. It was probably unscientific as all hell. McNair, no doubt, would have a better explanation and who was he to argue with the man? How it looked to him and how it probably was being two different things. Boyd figured that was probably true.

"Lookit this one," Maki said. "A freaking crocodile, eh?"

McNair and Jurgens came over, looking at what appeared to be the near-complete fossil skeleton of a reptile maybe twenty feet in length.

"Good God," McNair said, down on his hands and knees next to it. "This is a therapsid. And a big one, too."

"What's that?" Maki said.

"Therapsids were reptiles that mammals eventually developed from. Some were vegetarians and some were carnivores." He examined the skull, the teeth jutting from it. "Look at these canines and incisors, this one was a carnivore."

There were more bones scattered about. Lots of them. McNair identified some belonging to fish and others from therapsids, some quite large and others from smaller rodent-like forms. He went on and on in dusty detail about life in the late Permian and the massive extinction that wiped most of it out.

"This area must be part of some ancient headland," he said. "Where the sea met the land. Incredible. We're probably standing on a beach from the Upper Permian."

Breed got bored and wandered off by himself. He disappeared over a rise and they could see his light bobbing about.

"Hey!" he called out. "There's pillars over here."

That got everyone scrambling to take a look.

They all arrived about the same time and saw an uneven expanse of ground stretching away as far as their lights would reach. It was set with low mounds and sloping hills. And everywhere... pillars. Not just two or three, but hundreds stretching away in all directions. Some were narrow like pipes and others had very wide bases that gradually tapered as they moved up and up, many right into the living rock far above. They were set in stands, crowded together so tightly you would have had to turn sideways to get between them, while others occupied low hillocks above.

McNair started moving around them, touching them and muttering under his breath.

Boyd moved with him, puzzled by what he was seeing. When Breed said "pillars" he was thinking of something out of classical architecture, Doric columns and the like. But these were nothing like that. Their surfaces were rough and set with overlapping scales and sometimes little thorns. It all reminded him of the skin of pineapples.

"They look kind of like trees," he finally said.

"They are trees," McNair said, nearly breathless with it all. "Permian trees. Good God in heaven, a forest of trees, still rooted, still in their upright living positions after 250 million years."

Breed and Maki looked at each other.

"Doc," Breed said, knocking on one of them. "They're made of stone."

"They're petrified," Boyd said. "Just like those bones. They're fossils."

"Exactly," McNair said.

All of them got the significance of it now: a forest of prehistoric trees.

And there had to be hundreds of them.

As they explored around, they found some that were no taller than a man and others that must have been eighty feet when they were alive, and still others that were probably hundreds of feet that disappeared right into the rock overhead. Some were just trunks, others had been snapped off thirty feet up, petrified logs and branches and deadfalls lying about. But many were nearly intact, their limbs still extant. Not only had the trees themselves been fossilized, but the loam around them. Heaps of fallen leaves were as petrified as the trees they fell from.

Boyd found it hard to take it all in, that immense, maze-like run of trees like the masts of ships.

Maki just didn't get it, though. "How does a tree turn to rock?"

Breed said, "It's like out in Arizona, the Petrified Forest. I been there. Ain't you ever heard of that, Maki?"

"Oh yeah, sure."

McNair told them that the trees in the Petrified Forest in Arizona were from the Triassic, but what they had here was much older. Much, much older. In Arizona, some of the trees were still rooted as these, but many had been washed by prehistoric seasonal floods into sandy river channels where they were buried in gravel and sand rich in volcanic ash.

"The process is called permineralization," McNair explained. "I imagine this entire area was in some sort of lowland swamp or valley during the Permian. A flash flood probably turned that valley into a bog or a muddy lake. Hence, oxygen which causes oxidation and rot, was kept away. These trees were buried in water and sediment. What happens next is that the trees either disintegrate or are compressed into coal over a period of millions of years, or, in this case, they permineralize. Minerals gradually replace the woody tissues and you have petrified trees."

Breed said, "Yeah, but this is better than the Petrified Forest. A lot better."

"Yes. Yes, it is. This entire forest must have been locked in that bog and the entire thing, through the passage of thousands or even hundreds of thousands of years must have dried up, but the sediment that enclosed it turned to stone, capturing our forest as we now see it. Nearly intact."

McNair said that much later, whatever geologic upheaval swallowed up the Permian strata and sank it deep into Precambrian rock, brought the forest here as well. Through the ages, waters must have eroded the rocks away and exposed what they were seeing now.

Maki was interested. "There's nothing like this anywhere? Not even Arizona?"

McNair shook his head. "A few years ago, a nice stand of petrified Permian trees were discovered near the Beardmore Glacier in Antarctica. But nothing like this."

Some of them rose up out of the rock on spidery tangles of fossilized roots and others had trunks so huge that three men could not have circled them with their arms. McNair said there were both conifers and deciduous trees in this forest. They were looking at cycads and gymnosperms and seed ferns, an amazing variety. He pointed out short trees with fern-like fronds that were called Archaeopteris, the progenitors of modern pines. Something called a Dicroidium that looked more like a large houseplant than a tree. There were primitive Ginkgoes with broad, fanlike leaves, cycads that looked much like palm trees, and Glossopteris, another seed fern, but very treelike in appearance. This species had a massive trunk that tapered gradually upward maybe fifty or sixty feet where a cluster of whipping branches sprouted. The huge, broad leaves in the rock were Glossopteris leaves, McNair said.

He squatted next to a wide stump, examining the rings within which were bright and sparkling with mineral deposits of many colors. "Look here," he said. "If I had a mass spectrometer, I could identify these minerals, but I'm prepared to make a guess. Much of this is quartz, but the various trace elements give the petrified wood its color. Copper and chrome oxide create greens and blues, iron oxide gives us reds and browns and yellows, aluminum silicates produce whites, etc. etc."

Boyd, for one, was ignoring the lecture.

It was interesting stuff and any other time he might have listened intently, but not down here. Not in the bowels of the earth in the enshrouding darkness with nothing but the sound of dripping water and echoing voices to break that heavy, humming silence. It was like a graveyard and he honestly did not like it. It was meant to stay buried and he wished to God it had. He panned his light around, all those fossilized tree trunks leaning and canting this way and that, clustered together, crowded like the spokes of bike tires. The flashlight beam created sliding, distorted shadows and made the trees look like they were in motion. More than once, he was certain that something had moved out there in that cemetery of pillars and monuments.

It was imagination. It had to be.

Yet, that feeling in his guts was expanding, filling him with an oily blackness, drowning him in his own mounting claustrophobia and paranoia. This place had not known light or air in eons and the idea of that disturbed him in ways he could not adequately catalog. Like maybe this hermetically sealed graveyard might start waking up at any moment, unleashing all its terrible secrets after 250 million years.

That was crazy, of course.

But as he wiped sweaty dew from his brow, he could not dismiss it entirely. Because ever since they'd reached the petrified forest he'd had the feeling that they were being watched.

# 9

Twenty minutes later—after climbing through those close-packed trunks, navigating petrified logs, and fields of four-foot stumps wider than oval tabletops—they waded through a pool of freezing water and pressed through another stand of trees and what they saw on the other side literally took their breath away.

"Those ain't trees," Maki said. "That's...that's a city..."

"Can't be," Breed said. "Not down here."

Boyd reserved judgment, as did McNair and Jurgens. They stepped forward, trying to make sense of what they were seeing. At first glance, sure, it did look like some sort of city, though maybe village would have been more accurate. Not buildings exactly, but trees. Immense things like California redwoods spread out and each bigger around than the opening to a train tunnel. About forty or fifty feet up, they had been sheared off flat, giving the impression of flat-roofed, man-made structures. Like the others they were completely turned to stone, but unlike the others they were honeycombed with oval openings, dozens and dozens of them.

Boyd thoughtthat, yes, it did look like a village of sorts with gigantic trees used as buildings, but no ordinary village. This was primeval looking, weird and offbeat like those monkey villages in *The Planet of the Apes*. You just couldn't imagine men living in places like this, climbing up into those holes and kicking off their shoes. If those cells were indeed domiciles of some sort, they looked like the sort some simian tree dwellers might fashion. Maybe even Tarzan.

"Those are trees," Jurgens said.

McNair nodded. "Yes...but immense. I've never heard of anything like this from the Permian."

"Maybe they're not from the Permian," Breed said.

"They have to be," McNair pointed out. "I mean, it would be a little coincidental to assume that these were far older, that they had been standing petrified in our theoretical valley when the flood claimed the rest of this forest. It would be stretching."

He and Jurgens walked around with their lanterns and long-handled flashlights while the others just stood and stared. There were at least a dozen of the big trees, some up on mounds, and some down in little draws sitting in standing water. They led right up to the far wall of the cavern where at some time in the past there had been a cave-in, swallowing the rest of the petrified Permian world. Set amongst them, were dozens of the other trees.

Breed kept panning his light around, studying them. "I don't know, Doc," he said when McNair returned. "These big ones just look...I don't know..."

"Older," Maki said.

And Boyd was with them on that. Like this was a sacred grove that had been abandoned, all the little trees inserting themselves and growing wild when whoever or whatever cut those cells was long, long gone. Regardless, there was something eerie about them standing so big and stark, like monoliths and monuments. The flashlight beams scanning them made the cell mouths seem to move as shadows spilled from them.

Jurgens and McNair went up to one and started peering inside it. Boyd and Breed followed suit. The openings were all about four-feet in diameter. Inside, were little cells maybe five-feet high by ten long. You could still see the chopping marks in the petrified wood. McNair climbed inside one and examined this.

"It looks like this was done when the tree was still alive," he said.

"But by who?" Breed said. "I mean, who was around 250 million years ago to hollow out these little apartments?"

Jurgens shook his head. "It wasn't a matter of *who*, Breed, but *what*. There were no people during the Permian. This is, was, the work of some arboreal creature. Some tree-living species that chewed these cavities open."

"They remind me of those holes the prairie dogs dig in their sand piles at the zoo," Maki said.

"What could have made these, Doc?" Boyd asked.

"I...I'm not sure," McNair said. "But it's apparent that there were very many of them and it must have taken time."

Boyd looked into another. "Almost looks like toolwork, don't it?" he said, putting his flashlight beam on the meticulously carved ceiling, the series of hack marks that looked like maybe they'd been done with an axe.

"It wasn't done by tools," McNair said, but he didn't sound convinced of that himself.

"But what cut them off flat on top, Doc?" Breed wanted to know.

McNair said, "There's no way of telling. Could have been that they grew that way or some natural force did it. The movement of the rock above may have sheared them off over a period of millions of years. Hard to say."

"Almost looks like it was done on purpose," Maki said.

Boyd stood before the nearest tree, sweeping his light up it, counting all the cells set into its face. They went right up to the very top. Dozens of them. Looking at them, he was reminded of a bee honeycomb. Whatever lived in them must have been a very good climber.

McNair was taking photograph after photograph.

"Well, gentlemen, I think we should call it a day," Jurgens said. "No sense waiting around down here until our batteries go dead."

Boyd was in perfect agreement with that. This was plenty for one day. Let the scientists figure this all out. He wanted to get topside again, get out of the cavern and the mines in general, suck in some air that wasn't dank and stagnant smelling.

*After this I'm gonna need a drink,* he thought, *maybe four or five of them. In fact, I just might—*

Maki, who had been investigating trees ahead, came running back, shining his light around up in the air. "What the hell was that?"

They all looked at him.

In the glow of the lanterns, his face had taken on the color of yellow cheese. His eyes were wide and white, his lips pulled away from his teeth.

"I didn't hear anything," Jurgens said.

But nobody was saying it was his imagination. They were all looking around them now as if the unpleasant possibility that they might not be alone down there had just occurred to them. Flashlight beams scanned about, but no one heard anything but that continual, morose dripping of water. The air smelled like it had been blown from a crypt...yellow bones and flaking shrouds, dust and advanced age.

"I heard it," Maki said. "Up there…up on one of those trees. A kinda scratching sound."

# 10

All flashlights went up.
Beams arced through the darkness.

There were lots of the other trees around them, the gymnosperms and cycads standing about like posts. Some were fifty feet in height and the flashlights played about their tops.

"There's nothing up there, Maki," Jurgens said.

"Wait," Breed said. "I heard something, too."

Then they all did. A knocking sound like a woodpecker working a dead tree. It had that same hollow, continual rapping. It went on for maybe five seconds, stopped, then started again. It was coming from high above, from the apex of one of the trees... but they could see nothing up there.

"Fuck is that?" Breed said.

McNair swallowed. "I assumed this cavern was sealed, but something could have gotten in through a crevice. Bats, maybe."

"I never heard bats knock like that," Maki pointed out.

Boyd stood there, his heart pounding and the cylinder of the flashlight in his hand feeling very greasy like it might slide out of his fist at any moment.

Jurgens cleared his throat. "Well, let's get on our way—"

"Shut up," Breed said.

They were hearing noises now. Not just that knocking, but a scraping sound from high above them like tenpenny nails were being scratched over petrified wood. A flurry of noise that went on for maybe thirty seconds. Then nothing. Nothing at all.

"There's something up there," Breed whispered, like he was afraid that whatever it was might hear him.

All lights went up into the petrified treetops again. Most were just posts lacking branches. The lights swept over them and there was absolutely nothing up there. Nothing that the lights could find.

The sounds started again, knocking and scraping, not from one particular tree, but from many as if whatever was up there was leaping from tree to tree over their heads. It stopped again and they all stood there, silent and motionless, sensing something but not knowing what it was. Boyd's flashlight was shaking in his hand, his beam jumping around. He wanted badly to run, to get the hell out of there, before whatever it was showed. Because he had a bad feeling that it was about to. That whatever was up there was about to drop down amongst them in a flurry of scratching limbs.

What they heard next was a clicking.

*Click, click, click.*

The sound of a deathwatch beetle in the wall of a deserted house or a cicada up in a gum tree. Just that repetitive, chitinous clicking like some insect rubbing its forelegs together or tapping them on its carapace. Whatever it was, it was not a good sound and nobody dared speak. Dared acknowledge what they were hearing.

*It's like Morse Code*, Boyd thought. *Like something up there is trying to communicate with us.*

"I'm getting the fuck out of here," Maki said.

But he didn't move. What came next stopped him dead.

In fact it stopped them all dead and took away any slim hope they had that what was up there was a bat or something ordinary. It started as a low whistling sound and built to a screeching, strident piping that went right up their spines. It sounded frenzied, desperate, the shriek of some mountain cat crying out in agony and despair and maybe even stark melancholy. It rose up to a shrill cacophony and then slowly faded. And by then, they were all scared.

Nothing with a voice like that could by remotely normal or remotely sane.

Boyd stood there, trying to pull air into his lungs. He could not get past the idea that there was an almost feminine caliber to that cry. Anguished, haunted, and demented, but somehow female. Like some big and hideous insect imitating a human cry. The idea of that made his flesh crawl in waves. It was not a human voice or even a tone a human would be capable of producing, yet it was not strictly bestial and there was no denying a certain sorrow in its pitch.

But it was enough.

It was plenty.

"Let's get the hell out of here," Jurgens said and the desperation in his voice was real.

They made it maybe ten feet before things started to happen.

The earth below and above them rumbled like a hungry belly and things began to move and shake and tremble. Rocks and dust fell from overhead. The prehistoric trees began to sway back and forth. Everything was in motion, including the men who tried to stay on their feet. Lights went spinning in all directions as their owners pitched this way and that.

"A cave-in!" Breed called out. "A fucking cave-in!"

Boyd hit the ground, waiting for millions of tons of rock to come down on top of him, for the lot of them to be squashed flat like his old man in the Mary B. mine. He heard that rumbling from the distance and realized that whatever was happening, it was apparently not happening in the cavern. Rocks were falling and dust was kicked up, but the real thunder came from the distance. And then a shock wave rolled at them, throwing everyone to the ground. In the glow of a dropped lantern, he saw one of those giant stone trees sway back and forth and come right down on top of him. He felt the impact as its trunk trapped his leg with a white-hot rush of pain.

And in the back of his head, a voice said, *yer probably the only guy ever crushed by a falling tree out of the Permian.*

Then there was darkness.

# 11

Up in Level #8, it was a dog and pony show and Russo, the mine captain, didn't expect much more. But he was there, hell yes, cracking the whip and kicking ass because time was a factor here. Those men were down there. Trapped. Maybe dead, but maybe alive and this was what he was counting on. It was what everyone was counting on. The brass at Hobart were having kittens over this one and they were crawling up Russo's ass. They were so far up there he could feel them in the back of his throat.

And what he got, he gave.

Standing there in his rainsuit, boots, and miner's helmet, he was watching the diggers clearing rubble from the drift. They were going at it hard, but not hard enough for Russo's liking. "C'mon! C'mon, you fucking pussies! Clean that drift! We got to get it blasted out to get that drilling rig in! Move! Move! Christ, you boys dig like I fuck!"

It was a hive of activity down there with the clearing and the blasting, the rubble being carted away. But the brass were on him and he had never let them down before and he wouldn't let them down now.

They wanted action.

They wanted results.

There were families out there who wanted to know what the hell was going on and what was being done to free their men. They were riding the Hobart people hard and when they hopped off the saddle, the Safety and Mine people hopped on. And topside, Jesus, the media were already descending and interviewing family members and word had it they'd already dug up a few old hands that were more than happy to spill the beans about the unsafe working conditions at the Hobart. Russo knew who those guys were…people like Lem Rigby and Charlie DeCock. Men he'd fired for being lazy, careless, or downright incompetent. Here was their chance to bask in the sun and point fingers and, goddamn yes, they were sure pointing them.

Revenge, that was it.

Against the Hobart mine. Against Russo himself.

And Russo, like every man who'd worked those drifts and channels, knew that the word of those guys wasn't worth a sip of piss on a hot day, but the media didn't know that. The journalists and TV parasites didn't know the difference between a stope and a gopher hole, just like they didn't know the difference between a hard-working man and a guy like Lem Rigby who'd shown up drunk and been canned on the spot by Russo.

No, they didn't know what Rigby's game was.

They only knew that in him and half-wit Charlie DeCock they had eyewitnesses to the workings of the mine itself that would sweeten the deal and make the Hobart look guilty as hell. And already the brass were smelling lawsuits and they did not care for the stink.

Russo knew somebody would get dragged over the rocks on this one.

And that somebody would probably be him.

So, he shouted. He yelled. He threatened and intimidated and raised three kinds of holy hell.

But what he was thinking about all the while was not his job and not lawsuits and not those candyass reporters topside.

He was thinking about Jurgens and the miners.

Down in the darkness, far below.

Russo had been trapped underground for thirty-six hours once, so he knew. He goddamn well knew what that score was.

As the air hammers chiseled and the rubble was dragged out, as hydraulic lines vibrated and steam hoses hissed and men scrambled, he said under his breath, "Don't worry, boys. I'll get you out. Johnny Russo is on the job and I'll get your fine white asses out of the pit. See if I don't. And if you're nothing but corpses, by God, then I'll carry you out with my own bare hands."

# 12

Boyd came awake from a dream where he was crushed beneath a mountain of solid rock gasping and clawing out, his face beaded with cold, sour-smelling sweat.

"Easy now," a voice said.

Breathing fast, he found that he was laying on his back, his leg from the knee down numb and rubbery feeling. He could see the glow of the lanterns, but they were dimming fast. He blinked his eyes and tried to speak, but all that came out was a groaning sound.

"He's coming around," Breed said.

"Take it easy," Jurgens told him. "One of those goddamn trees caught your leg. We got it off you, but you got a nasty compound fracture, son. Don't try and move."

But, of course, Boyd did and right away the pain kicked in. It felt like somebody was driving a spike into his shin. He let out a little muted scream and settled back down again.

"Take it easy now," Jurgens told him. "You're going to be fine. We'll get you out of here."

Maki let out a high little laugh. "No shit, Jurgens? And how do you plan on doing that? How do you plan on getting us out of this fucking tomb? Huh?" He shook his head. "Let me be the first to clue you in on something, Boyd. We're trapped down here. We're trapped in this fucking cavern—"

"Shut the hell up," Breed told him.

"—and we can't get out. We get to sit around and twiddle our fucking thumbs while our lights go out and the air goes bad. How's that for kicks, Boyd? How's that for company incentive?"

"Swear to God," Breed said, "you don't pipe down, I'll kick the living shit out of you right now."

"We'll be fine," Jurgens said. "Even now they'll be digging to get us out."

They were all sitting around him in a little circle by lantern light and Boyd looked from face to face to face. None of them looked particularly hopeful. Jurgens told him that the cave-in had sealed the stope leading out of the cavern. But that was no real reason for concern, because the cavern was huge and it would no doubt take weeks and weeks to use up all the oxygen in there. And long before that, they'd be dug out. Boyd listened and didn't honestly believe a word of it. Maybe if it was just the stope that had caved-in and the tunnel leading to it and even the spider hole from the drift above...maybe then, they'd actually get dug out. But what if it was more than that? What if it was Level #8 above? What then? Then getting to the cavern would take months maybe.

The only good thing, he supposed, was that Jurgens had called up to the drift with his walkie-talkie every fifteen minutes. He had told the men above about the stope they found and the cavern it led to. That was something and under the circumstances, it would have to be enough.

After a time, Boyd said, "How about those sounds?"

"We haven't heard anything else," McNair said.

Maki laughed again and it was a bad sort of laughter, the sort that echoed from a mind on the verge of a nervous breakdown. No one had ever doubted who the weak link in their chain was. But then again, they had not imagined a scenario like this that would put it to the test.

"Nope, not a thing," Maki said. "But I been feeling things."

"That's enough," Jurgens told him.

But Maki's days of kissing the guy's ass were long gone. "Well, who we kidding here, Jurgens? You know there's something out there same as I do. We all feel it out there, we just can't see it. But it's there and you all goddamn well know it. Something's out there. Something's watching us. And whatever in the fuck it is, we're trapped down here with it—"

But that's as far as he got in his little paranoid monologue because Breed's fist smashed into his face and dropped him like a dead tree.

Breed was one of the mellowest guys you'd want to meet. Boyd had known him only a matter of hours, but that much was apparent. But all this was too much...even for him. Maki wouldn't quit running his mouth and this was where it had gotten him.

"You think we need to listen to your shit, Maki?" Breed said, on his feet and advancing on the downed man. "You think we need that? You think we ain't got enough fucking problems right now?"

Maki opened his mouth to say something else and Breed went right at him. No one tried to intervene. Maybe, on some subconscious level, they were glad it was finally happening. Maki tried to rise, his mouth full of blood, and Breed let him. He let him find his feet and then he really gave it to him. A flurry of lefts and rights that knocked his head this way and that. Anyone of them would have put him down if it hadn't been for the blow that followed it, righting him again. Maki's nose rained blood and his left eye was nearly closed and his lip was split wide open.

"Please," he kept trying to say as Breed pummeled him. "Please...stop it...stop it...stop it..."

"Okay, I stopped," Breed said and gave him a shot in the belly that put him back down.

By then Jurgens was on his feet. "Knock it off, Breed! Jesus, you'll kill him."

Breed shook his head and sat back down, staring at Maki. Looking for a reason to really let loose on him. But Maki gave him none. He squatted there, dazed and punchy, spitting out blood and making a whimpering sound under his breath like a dog that had just been whipped with a newspaper.

"We have to keep our heads here," McNair finally said. "We can't let this go on."

"He's right," Jurgens said. "This is a bad spot, but they're going to get us out. What we need is something constructive to do in the meantime."

"Well, I'm open to suggestions," Breed said.

They all were. But what, really, was there to do? What could possibly take their minds off the fix they were in or the possibility of the unpleasant deaths they might soon be facing?

But Jurgens had that covered. "Listen to me," he said. "All of you. Now I know the drill. I know what's going on up there right now. They've mobilized every possible resource to reach us. And they will, believe me, they will. But maybe we ought to think about helping out. We know the stope leading into this cavern caved-in, but we have no way of knowing the extent of it. There might just be a wall of rocks between us and freedom. I say we form up, go back there and get to work. What do you say?"

Breed stood up. "I'm for it. I can't stand sitting around like this."

"Okay, then. Maki? You stay here with Boyd. I'll go with Dr. McNair and Breed, get them started, then I'll come back. They'll dig first for a couple hours, then we'll take our turns."

"I guess that leaves me out," Boyd said.

That got a few weak chuckles, nothing more.

Maki had been sitting silently, nursing his wounds, but now he jumped up and swatted at the air. "Fuck was that?" he cried. "What the fuck was that?"

"What the hell's he talking about?" Breed said.

McNair and Jurgens watched him as he spun around in the lantern light, swatting at the air.

Jurgens said, "Calm down, Maki. Jesus, there's nothing. You're imagining things."

Maki was breathing so hard it seemed he might hyperventilate. He kept brushing the back of his neck. "Something touched me."

Boyd felt a chill go up his spine at that. He'd thought, right before Maki freaked out, that he'd heard a funny scraping on the rocks. But he didn't dare say so.

Flashlight beams swung around, but there was only the dead trees and the rocks, nothing more.

"There's nothing, Maki," Jurgens said.

"There was, there was!" He licked his bloody lips and peered around suspiciously. "Something touched me. I don't give a fuck whether you believe me or not, but something touched the back of my neck."

"What?" Breed said.

"I don't know...it felt...it felt like a stick or something."

"Ain't no sticks down here."

Nobody was sure what to make of it, so nobody tried. They started talking about digging their way out, leaving Maki to his imagination and Boyd to wondering.

"I'll be back in a few minutes," Jurgens said.

Then he, Breed, and McNair walked off, taking one of the lanterns with them. God only knew how long the batteries would last, so for the time being everyone was just using the lights on their helmets. Even those were dimming steadily, casting a surreal, weird glow and making everyone aware of how dark it was down there.

When the footfalls of the digging party vanished away, Boyd said, "Maki? You okay?"

"Sure, I'm fine," he said. "I'm just fine. But I tell you what, Boyd, that fucking Breed is a dead man. He can't do this and get away with it."

"Worry about that later, after we get out of here," Boyd told him.

But Maki laughed. "Don't kid yourself, Boyd, ain't none of us getting out of here alive."

"Stop it," Boyd said. "Just stop that shit."

"It touched me," Maki said. "Whatever's down here, Boyd, it touched the back of my neck."

"Okay."

"It's got fingers."

"Maki—"

"They feel like sticks…like pencils."

Boyd waited, saying nothing.

# 13

While they waited, Boyd was not only thinking about his wife and the kid she was carrying that he might never see, but about Russo. He could see his pig-ugly face in his mind, see the scowl on his mouth, hear those words he'd said when he put him on the graveyard shift: *You ain't gonna get all girly and run off on me when things get tough and dirty below, are you?*

And right then, remembering how his old man had died in the Mary B. and faced that sort of death day after day without so much as a twitch of nerve, he said, "No sir. I'm up to it."

"What?" Maki said.

"Nothing. Just talking to myself."

"Well, maybe we shouldn't be talking."

"Yeah...and why's that?"

Maki looked at him and his eyes were practically luminous in his grimy, bruised face. "Because it uses too much fucking air."

"It would take a hundred men a month to use up the air in this cavern, Maki. And you know it." And to prove that, he pulled out a cigarette and lit it. "You got nothing to worry about."

Maki shifted a bit. "Well, then maybe there's other reasons."

"Such as?"

Maki licked his lips. "Because we ain't alone down here, you dumb shit. And the more we talk, the more what's out there will know where we are."

"Quit it. You sound like a kid scared of the fucking dark."

Maki moved, grabbing his arm. "I am scared, cookie. I'm real scared and you should be, too."

Of course, Boyd was scared. Scared like he'd never been before in his life. Even more scared than he'd been when news had reached him about his old man dying down in the Mary B. That had been a fear of the future and a fear of going through life without his old man's smiling face, his salty wit, his unflappable demeanor which could weather any storm as long as they were together, as long as he had his family. That had been a fear of closure and a fear of what it would do to his sisters and particularly his mother. But even as bad as that fear had been as he laid in his bed the night of the funeral, the wind making the roof creak, he knew that it was done with. Over. That he could cry his eyes out every night and withdraw from life and make this hard on his mom...but it was over.

But this fear...it was now.

It was happening.

Nothing was over, it was still rolling along. There was something out there and he knew it and that knowledge was not only terrible, but crushing. Just them. And something in that cavern. Something unnatural.

In the distance, he could hear Breed and the others clearing rubble. Hear their voices echoing off into the darkness. He had never felt so small or so helpless in his life.

And then—

*Click, click, click.*

Christ, not again.

Boyd felt his entire body go tight as a wire. He felt like crying out or maybe getting up and running off even though there was nowhere to run to. And maybe he would have done both those things if it hadn't been for his bum leg and the fact that whatever was out there might hear him, might decide to come after him.

"You hear that?" Maki said, scared but also exhilarated.

"Sshhh!"

Maki didn't say a thing after that. He just pulled in a little closer to Boyd and did it most stealthily like a soldier in the jungle doing everything he could not to draw the attention of the enemy or a sniper's bullet. As he moved, something fell from his pocket and clattered to the ground.

It seemed very loud in the silence.

Boyd saw what it was...Maki's lock-blade knife. Maki picked it up again and then, offering him the most unpleasant of grins, tapped it against a stone near his knee. *Tap, tap, tap.*

The result was immediate.

Out in that cloying darkness: *click, click, click.*

God, that sound. Like a claw tapped against the trunk of one of those petrified trees. At that particular moment, Boyd could not imagine a worse sound to be hearing.

Maki raised the knife again.

"Don't," Boyd told him.

Maki tapped it against the stone…but changed the rhythm. This time it was *tap, tap, tap-tap-tap*. Boyd tensed at the sound of it, at Maki attempting to communicate with whatever in the hell was out there, hiding in the trees. For several seconds there was nothing, nothing at all. Boyd made to open his mouth to tell Maki he was an idiot, then:

*Click, click, click-click-click.*

Boyd felt his heart plummet as fear gouged a hollow inside him. He was so scared at that moment that it felt like a balloon was slowly expanding in his chest. Where the hell were Jurgens and the others? Why weren't they here to stop this madness before it went too far if it hadn't already?

*Tap-tap-tap-tap-tap, tap, tap*, went the knife.

And somewhere in that night world, the clicking sound repeated it exactly. Again and again, excitedly. It echoed through the cavern like fingernails tapping on the inside of a coffin lid. Boyd felt himself trembling. A trickle of cool sweat ran down his temple, cutting a clean path in his dirty face. The walkie-talkie was sitting but inches away and he desperately wanted to pick it up and call for help, get the others over here. Because he was trapped with a madman and with something far worse. Any moment now, he expected that horror to come whispering out of the foul blackness on a thousand legs.

But five minutes later, it still had not shown itself.

Boyd knew it wasn't over, though. He could feel it in his guts that now that they had communicated with it, it would never leave them alone. It would get more daring. It was curious now. Again, he was about to jump Maki for what he had done, but then he heard it out there, moving around. It was skittering. That was the only word to describe that ticking sound he heard, a skittering of many legs. It was running up one tree and down another, leaping from trunk to trunk. And that skittering noise…like dozens of scratching nails…seemed to be far distant, then very close. Off to the left, then the right. Moving away and then ominously coming right at them.

Maki and he were pressed up against one another like lovers now, needing each other's touch.

They looked around, their helmet spots darting around in the darkness but never finding anything but the spokes of those prehistoric trees.

"Fucking place is haunted," Maki said with absolute conviction.

Boyd did not argue with him: it was surely haunted, just not by ghosts as such. But at the same time, he could feel the atmosphere around him and it was charged with some ethereal energy, an oscillating discharge like static electricity.

The thing out there clicked again. Twice.

Maki did not dare answer it.

After a few seconds, it clicked again: *click, click, click-click-click.*

Maki made a low moaning sound in his throat.

The thing clicked and clicked, repeating the previous exchange perfectly. It wanted to communicate again, but the men were silent and as its repeated attempts went unanswered, it began to click feverishly out of what seemed anger or frustration, not just clicking now but knocking loudly against a petrified bole.

The sounds were very loud, echoing and echoing.

After maybe five minutes in which Boyd and Maki were nearly holding each other out of terror, the sounds ceased. The silence that followed was somehow worse, pregnant with nameless possibility. And then another sound came, like air blown over the mouth of a pop bottle. A steadily rising mournful wailing that was high-pitched and hysterical in tone. It got louder and louder like the night-call of some huge insect, then died away.

The very timbre of it made the fine hairs at the back of Boyd's neck stand up, made the flesh at his groin shrivel. Because although that shrilling was not remotely human, there was something despondent and melancholy about it.

"Hell is that?" Maki said.

"I don't know what she is."

"She?" Maki whispered. *"She?"*

It had been a slip of the tongue, but Boyd did not retract it. For the very sound of that crying voice had been very feminine somehow and that was sheer lunacy, yet the certainty of it remained. That thing out there…dear God…it was female.

They sat there quietly for some time and the only sounds now were the distant dripping of water and the noise of Jurgens, Breed, and McNair clearing more rubble from the stope mouth. And Maki breathing with a hoarse, frantic sound.

"What're we gonna do, Boyd? Fuck are we gonna do?"

"We're gonna wait for them above to get us out," he said. "Listen, Maki, I don't know what's down here with us, but just leave it be. Don't fool with it. Don't try and make sounds for it. Maybe it'll…I don't know, maybe it'll just go away."

But he didn't believe that, not for a moment.

Because it was still out there and, God help him, but he could feel its eyes on them.

# 14

They'd been at it a good six hours that was closer to seven and Russo was feeling the heat. It was coming from every direction—the media, the families, the mine execs. It felt like every damn last one of them was standing on his back. He rubbed his aching neck and swallowed a couple Tylenol. He watched the men widening the drift, the constant sound of jack hammers and rock drills, the hiss of steam and thudding of limestone chunks being shoveled into metal cars. It was all making his head pound.

He rubbed his eyes, then his temples.

Everything down here echoed. Banging and booming, clanging and ringing out. Russo lit a cigarette and motioned Corey, the shift boss, over.

"Well?" he said.

"We're making progress, but I'm guessing it'll take us most of the day to widen that drift so we can get the raise borer in here," Corey told him. "If that shaft is just filled up with loose limestone, we can drill through it like cheese, but…"

Russo glared at him. "But?"

Corey shook his head. "You know same as me. If it's just loose rubble, we can drill it in three, four hours with a reamer bit. Even cutting four-hundred feet we'll have her in eight hours…but we don't know what happened down there. Whole goddamn earth might have moved. Limestone is unstable. If we have to cut through solid rock it's gonna take days."

"And more likely weeks," Russo said, spitting.

Weeks. Weeks down there for chrissake. Russo pulled off his cigarette and watched Corey making his way up to the drift, hollering orders and telling the diggers to keep at it. He stood there, wondering what it was like for them down there. He remembered the time he'd been trapped below. Even now, it made his flesh crawl.

# 15

Boyd was waiting.

He didn't know for what or maybe he did and just didn't want to admit it to himself. He lay there next to the tree that had broken his leg. Maki hadn't spoken in some time and he figured that was a good thing. The silence was killing him, the desolation and the claustrophobia that clawed at his throat, but he did not want to know what was going on in Maki's head because he figured it was plenty bad.

Much like what was in his own head.

A sound.

Shit.

"What's that?" Maki said.

Then a light splashed through the spiderwebbing of trees and they saw Jurgens coming in their direction, moving over mounds of rock and down into little hollows, splashing through puddles. He leapfrogged a cluster of roots and stood before them, panting.

"We're making some progress, I think," he told them. "Lot of rock fall over there, but Breed and McNair are doing a good job of it. When they come back, Maki, we'll take our turn."

"Maybe she don't want us getting out," Maki said.

Jurgens looked at him, smiling as if he expected a good joke, but seeing that none was coming, he frowned. "What are you talking about?"

"The sounds," Boyd told him. "They came again."

"Yeah?"

"Worse."

"Click, click, click," Maki said.

Boyd told him what had happened, realizing how ridiculous it sounded, but he did not feel ridiculous telling it. Because the fear was still on him. He wore it like a skin.

"Could have been a weird echo," Jurgens told them. "I've heard some pretty strange subterranean echoes in my time."

Boyd shook his head. "It wasn't an echo. The same sounds repeated, but of a different caliber. And that other sound...that moaning or whatever in the Christ it was. It wasn't natural, not at all."

"Ghost," Maki said. "It sounded like a ghost going w-o-o-o-o-o-o-o..."

Jurgens didn't even comment on that. It was absurd. "Do you realize what you two are saying? Ghosts?"

No, no, no, Jurgens wasn't going to listen to bullshit like that and you could see it on his face. He was a mining engineer. He was the guy who cut shafts and found the raw ore that made others rich and kept industries rolling. *Ghosts*. Of all things. Maybe there were such things and maybe there weren't, but not down here. Not in this Paleozoic tomb. Because when you talked ghosts you were talking the spirits of dead men or women and no human beings had ever, ever set foot in here before them. If there was a ghost down here then it was the goddamned ghost of something that had died in the Permian.

"I don't believe in ghosts, mister, and if you do then you need your fucking head examined."

"Something's out there," Boyd said. "I heard it."

"What? Something alive? Something that survived for a quarter of a billion years in a hermetically-sealed cavern thousands of feet down? Good Christ, Boyd. Do you know what you're saying?"

"I guess not."

"But it's out there, Mister Hot-shit Engineer, and you heard it before, too," Maki said then and the tone of his voice was as near that of madness as either man had ever heard. "It's waiting out there, all right. It knows we're here. And I think before this is over we just might get to look it in the face."

Maki was sulking and Jurgens kept fiddling with his walkie-talkie like he honestly thought he could get a message above through all that goddamn rock. You could hear the distant sounds of Breed and McNair clearing away the rubble, the muted glow of their lantern coming through the forest of petrified trees.

"Boyd thinks it's a girl," Maki said.

Boyd sighed. "Shut the hell up."

Jurgen's looked up from his walkie-talkie. His face was stern in the glow of the lantern. "What the hell are you two talking about?"

"Talking about Boyd," Maki said. "And his girlfriend."

Boyd lit another cigarette and ignored him. He studied the trunks of the petrified trees and imagined what the forest must have looked like during the Permian when it was growing and green. He could almost feel the dead stagnant heat of the primordial jungle. The buzzing of ancient insects, things sliding through the underbrush. He blinked his eyes and saw only the graveyard spires and stone masts around him, the spoking shadows they threw in every direction.

Jurgens asked no more about what Maki said. Boyd had a pretty good idea that he just didn't want to know.

Then somewhere out in the darkness: *click, click, click.*

Boyd felt himself go stiff as board. Not again, Jesus, not again.

Maki made a pathetic sound under his breath that was part whimpering and part low, beaten laughter.

It came again, but louder: *CLICK, CLICK, CLICK.*

"It's her," Maki said.

They waited there, silent, motionless, each praying it would just go away. When Maki made to answer the sounds by tapping his knife, Jurgens grabbed his wrist and glared at him. Nobody made a move, a sound, anything. They waited there as stiffly as the petrified trees around them.

Then: *CLICK, CLICK, CLICK.*

Boyd was trembling. A cool and greasy sweat ran down his face. He felt something like a moan of utter despair building in his throat but he would not give it vent. He didn't dare.

Whatever was out there, it seemed to be growing impatient. *CLICK, CLICK, CLICK,* it sounded. *CLICKA, CLICKA, CLICKA-CLICK.* When that brought no response, it began pounding on the boles of the trees with a hollow knocking noise as if it was hitting them with a shaft of wood. *Bang, bang, bang. THUD-THUD-THUD.*

"She's getting mad," Maki said, his voice breaking.

"You're crazy," Jurgens told him.

But then it came again, that hammering and pounding. It was frantic in its desperation, beating on the stone trees, desperate, absolutely desperate for an answer, for anything.

When it had ended, echoing away into nothingness, Jurgens wiped sweat from his face with a hankie.

"She doesn't like to be ignored," Boyd told him.

# 16

B reed felt McNair grab his arm. "Quiet," he said.
   "What?"
"Quiet."
Breed listened. There was nothing for maybe five seconds, then a weird, distant droning sound rose up and died away. It sounded, if anything, like the continual buzzing of a summer locust.
"What the hell was that?"
"Quiet," McNair said again.
Breed gently set down the wedge of rock that was in his hands. He had a neckerchief wrapped around his mouth because they were kicking up so much dust digging through the rubble. Clouds of it drifted like fog in the light of the lantern. McNair's face was pale, his eyes huge and wet. His lower lip was trembling.
There was another noise now.
Something was circling around them out there, moving over the rocks with a ticking sound like a cat's claws will make on linoleum when they're not retracted. Tick, tick, tick, ticka-ticka-tick. Now the sounds stopped as if what had made them became aware that they were listening for it.
"What's that smell?" Breed said, pulling down his neckerchief.
But McNair shushed him. Whatever it was, it was thick in the air, a smell of age and dryness like the hot, dead stink of attics and sealed trunks. They both stood there, listening. Breed felt the sweat on his brow began to run down his cheeks. He licked his lips. He did not know exactly where their visitor was, but he could feel its nearness, sense its presence along his spine. He expected that any moment it would leap out at him, snarling and gibbering, a furry and elfin form with gnashing yellow teeth.
But that didn't happen.
It waited.
They waited.
He felt McNair's grip on his arm tighten and he knew why:

there was another sound, maybe one they'd been hearing for some time but not truly registering: a hollow sound of drawn-out respiration like wind sucked through a pipe.

It was the sound of breathing.

McNair moved very slowly, very carefully. He picked-up his long-handled flashlight from where it sat on a shelf of sandstone. He pointed it in the direction of the breathing. Dust was suspended in the beam like silt. He played it over the heaped rocks and pale green stalagmites rising up from the floor of the cavern like fangs. Shadows jumped and slid around them.

But there was nothing out there.

Nothing at all.

"Jurgens? Maki?" he called out and the fear in his voice was so thick, so tightly-wrapped, it was nearly strangling him. "If you're out there, call out for the love of God…"

Breed stood there. He was shaking. Listening to the breathing that blended into the immense stark silence of the catacombs around them in a perfect unbroken weave. Dead air seemed to scream in his ears. His flesh was actually crawling, his mouth dry, his belly pulled up into his chest.

And it was at that precise moment that he heard it.

That they both heard it.

A high, sweet singing that was scratching and tuneless, a repetitive sound of hysteria like a song of mourning sung by a madwoman over the graves of her children. It rose up in an unearthly shrill cadence then became the drone of a grasshopper in a summer field, growing louder and louder—then it cut out completely, echoing off into the subterranean depths.

Breed nearly fell over. He was hot and cold, his limbs rubbery, white-hot fingers of absolute primal dread sliding through his chest…and then, whatever was out there, was moving in their direction. *Tick, tick, ticka, ticka, ticka.* The sounds a wolf spider would make as it stalked its prey if the human ear were sensitive enough to hear them.

Breed and McNair did not move.

They stood rooted to the spot, both sweating and trembling as it advanced on them. McNair's hand was shaking on the flashlight. The beam jumped up and down, strobing. He had to put both fists on it to steady it and even then, he was only partially successful. The beam cut into the darkness, slicing through the clouds of rock dust and that horrible dry stench became pungent and sickening in the air.

Breed could see something…an eldritch and terrible form given body by the swirling dust. He couldn't be sure how much of it he saw and how much he imagined. It was roughly the size of man. A semi-visible hunched-over thing, a hazy apparition speckled with dust. It was creeping at them on a dozen spindly legs. He saw reaching arms, an elongated head of undulant tendrils like a nest of writhing, loathsome snakes…and a distorted face: something with clustered pods of eyes.

Then it leaped at them, howling with black hate.

It took McNair first.

It split him from crotch to throat and by the time Breed wiped the blood out of his eyes, he saw it in the glow of the lantern. It was crouched over McNair's corpse which was bleeding out in a steaming red lagoon. It was spattered red, lapping up blood with juicy, slobbering sounds.

Then it raised its head.

Breed saw three puckering red mouths like blow holes open and shriek in his face with absolute elemental wrath.

Then he started screaming.

# 17

They heard it.

That same mournful, shrill piping echoing through the cavern. Right away, flashlights were in fists, beams of light searching and searching for the source of that terrible sound. But there was nothing but the honeycombed trunks and the hundreds of petrified trees rising up around them like the mineralized columns of some primal amphitheater. The lights threw a lot of long, narrow shadows around, but nothing else.

Nothing else at all.

"Ain't nothing up there!" Maki said, his voice nearly delirious. "Not a goddamn thing! She's there but she isn't there!"

He was right, of course, and Boyd knew why. The thing making that sound was nowhere near them; it was with Breed and McNair now. As proof of that, they heard the first scream. It was high and wavering and fragmented and it was truly hard to say which of them made it. Only that it sounded out, a cry of absolute agony that was somehow animalistic and keening like an animal being tortured to death, then it was silenced with a wet, gurgling sound that echoed through the cavern.

Maki was crouched next to Boyd now, rocking back and forth on the balls of his feet, making a low moaning sound in his throat. When his voice came, it was almost a girlish whisper: *"It's killing them, Boyd! It's killing them now! Tearing them apart and then...then it'll come for us."*

Jurgens was on his feet, completely overwhelmed by it all. He was the man in charge. He was a leader of men...but now all that was gone and he was completely empty with its passing. His decision-making skills had been squashed flat and he did not know what to do. He moved this way, then that, cursing under his breath and breathing very hard.

Out in the darkness, there was a chittering sound.

Jurgens wiped sweat from his face. He thumbed the walkie-talkie because he had to. "Breed…McNair," he said into the mic, his voice very low and guarded. "Can you hear me? Can you hear me? *Breed! Goddammit! Answer me! Answer me!*"

But there was nothing but the futile sound of his own voice echoing away, submerging into the utter blackness of the cavern.

He looked at the other two men, shook his head, and started walking off. There was a look of absolute defeat on his face as if he'd played his best card and had still lost and there was no point in pretending now.

"Jurgens!" Boyd said. "You can't go out there! For chrissake, whatever's it is, it's trying to draw us out!"

Jurgens wiped his mouth with the back of his hand. "I have to do something," he said in a calm and controlled voice.

"Let him go, Boyd," Maki said, enjoying all this now maybe a little too much. "Let the big man go! Let him run out there and then we can listen to him die, too!"

The chittering rose and fell in regular cycles like crickets enjoying a summer's night. Only this sound was not crickets, it was too sharp, too piercing, too loud and completely unnatural to be anything as simple as an insect.

"Listen," Boyd said. "Listen."

Not the chittering now, but the sound of feet running. Running in their direction. Boyd didn't know what was out there, but he was pretty sure it did not have feet as such.

Jurgens clicked on his flashlight, put the beam out there to meet whatever was coming. They all saw a vague shape darting and stumbling through a stand of petrified trees. A big shape. Had to be Breed. He was running, looking frantically about him, making a low grunting with the exertion.

"Breed!" Jurgens called out. "Over here, over here!"

That chittering rose up again, becoming that same strident, inhuman piping. It grew in volume, nearly unbearable like a thousand forks scraped over a thousand blackboards. Breed fought free of the trees and something took him. Took him very fast. One moment he was coming and the next something had him, yanking him up into the air faster than Jurgens' flashlight beam could follow. He let out a wild, whooping scream and then there was a splattering sound like he'd been broken and squeezed out.

"Jesus," Jurgens said.

His flashlight beam could find nothing out there. But the posts of those ancient trees were sprayed red and running with blood. You could hear it dripping, landing with a slow plopping sound.

Jurgens lost it. He tossed his walkie-talkie and started shouting: "McNair! McNair! Breed! You answer me right goddamn now, do you hear me! YOU FUCKING BETTER ANSWER ME! BREED! MCNAIR!"

There was silence for maybe ten seconds while everyone held their breath, curled up into themselves, knowing that what was out there was not only weird and scary, but lethal and devastating.

And then another sound came: that same shrill screeching rising up louder and louder, sounding not only eerie and inhuman, but positively bleak and deranged. It rose and fell and then it did the worst possible thing. It mocked Jurgens with a scratching, mewling sound: "*Breeeeeeed! Breeeeeed!*" it squealed. "*Meeeek—naaaaaar!*"

"Oh my Christ," Jurgens said, going right down on his ass.

That horrible sound echoed away and then there was nothing. Nothing but the darkness gathering around them, concealing nameless things and mutant horrors that cried out in mewling, insane voices.

But Boyd had heard the caliber of it again: female. Not the voice of an adult, but the squealing voice of a little girl.

They all huddled there together in the circle of light and not a one of them thought of moving.

Boyd was thinking of Linda at home, waiting there at the kitchen table with some big breakfast she had prepared to celebrate his first graveyard shift. The eggs would be long cold by now, the pancakes mired in rubbery syrup, the bacon congealed with grease. Alone, scared, she would be waiting by the phone, eight months pregnant and expecting the very worst.

And in his mind, he said: *I'm sorry, baby. I'm so fucking sorry. I had a bad feeling about this, but I didn't get out while I could. And now… oh dear God…now you're going to be alone and our baby will never know its father.*

The tears filled his eyes, breaking hot and wet over his cheeks. His belly knotted up with frustration over it all, over the ugly, black death he was going to die down here in the womb of the earth itself. It was unfair. It was so goddamned unfair.

Maki uttered a low, desperate laugh. "I wonder who it'll get first, cookie. Me or you. Maybe Jurgens."

"Shut up."

But Maki, being Maki, did not shut up and maybe by that point he didn't even know how. "It's got us where it wants us," he breathed. "Whatever that thing is. Whatever we've woken up down here after a million, million years. It has us where it wants us and we're just meat, nothing but meat now."

"Shut the fuck up," Boyd told him, because, by God, compound fracture or no, if that whiny, beaten, gutless little weasel did not shut his mouth and shut it soon, he was going to wrap his hands around his fucking neck and squeeze until his eyeballs popped out of his head.

"Sure, cookie. Hee, hee. I'm quiet as a mouse."

Boyd laid there, breathless, terrified, waiting for that thing to come, knowing it had been down here all these many, many eons. A nightmare out of the Permian. Had it waited alone for 250 million years in the darkness? Was that even remotely possible? Or had it simply woken from cold dormancy when the air filled the dusty silence of the chamber and ended its 250 million year nap? He would never know and could not possibly conceive of an answer with his feverish mind. He only knew horror and absolute terror that was physical and crushing.

Just as he knew that what was out there was female.

And it was lonely.

That's why it had killed Breed and McNair. They were trying to tunnel out, trying to leave it to the darkness again and it couldn't have that. Not again. That's why it had tried to communicate by tapping and knocking on the petrified trees. It wanted them to answer back, to acknowledge its presence. There was no way he could know these things, yet he was certain of them. This thing was a horror from the Permian age, something that left no fossilized prints or bones, no clue to its existence or identity for paleontologists to scratch their gray heads over. It was something from the cellar of evolution, a grotesque thing that lived in the shadows of a primeval age. Something that channeled out honeycombed warrens in the immense stumps of primordial trees.

Yes, Boyd knew these things.

Just as he knew they'd be safe if they did not try to leave her. If they stayed, they would be fine, but if they panicked and threatened to entomb her with the mummified relics of her age, she would kill them. He could not know what she was or by what insane circumstances she had survived. But she had. Again, he thought that somehow she must have woken when air rushed into the Permian underworld. Dormant, perhaps, locked in some unbelievable hibernation. That had to be it, unless she had actually been awake down here the entire time. Aware of the passage of millions of years, that awful dead train of time. What would that be like? Trapped in this place, alone in a world turned to stone, alone in the darkness while your mind went to a screaming stew of waste? If that were the case, she would be deranged beyond imagining.

*No, I can't conceive of that*, Boyd told himself. *Such a thing could not be possible. She must have wakened when the air broke the seal of her tomb. It has to be something like that. She woke down here in the darkness, alone, frightened, confused and probably quite mad.*

If such a thing as her could know madness.

She probably wasn't dangerous, really, as long as they didn't threaten her with another eternity of solitude. Somehow, they had to communicate with her, give her the company she needed.

Jurgens stood up, shining his flashlight in every direction. "Keep away from us, you hear me? Whatever in the fuck you are, you better keep away from us! You come by us again and we'll kill you! Do you understand? Do you fucking understand me?"

"Don't," Boyd told him. "Don't do that...don't threaten her."

"*BREEEEEEEEEED!*" came the wailing voice. "*MEEEEK—NAAAAAAR!*"

Maki was sobbing under his breath. "It's a ghost," he was saying. "We're trapped down here with a ghost."

Boyd was going to tell him he was wrong, but maybe he wasn't. There was no way you could catalog that thing. Maybe it was alive and maybe it wasn't. Either way, Maki was right: she was a shadow, a wraith from antiquity.

The chittering rose up again and it was very close now.

Jurgens moved in a circle. "Get the fuck away from us!"

Maki was with him now, brandishing his flashlight like a weapon.

"Don't," Boyd said. "Dear Christ, don't do that..."

What seemed mere feet away, she let out a whining, pathetic shriek of utter agony and desolation and loneliness. The sound terrified Boyd and mainly because he heard the desperation in her voice, the cold cawing of millions of years that had scraped her mind raw. But Jurgens and Maki did not understand that. She was just a monster and they planned to deal with her as men had always dealt with monsters.

They ran at the direction of her voice and it was the worst thing they could have done. Maybe she did not understand the hateful things they called out to her or the threats they made, not in words, but she understood the tone. She knew she was threatened and she responded accordingly.

Boyd saw it happen and was powerless to stop it.

Something incredibly fast and unseen hit Jurgens. Hit him hard, tearing his throat out with a spray of meat and blood that splashed against the petrified trees and struck Boyd in the face, hot and steaming. Before Maki could utter so much as a cry of surprise, she took him, too. Boyd heard something thud into him and he was yanked high up into the air like a meat hook had caught him between the shoulder blades. Boyd heard him scream from the tops of the trees. A scream that was silenced by something wet shoved into his mouth. And then—

Boyd saw a blur of movement and Maki's corpse landed not four feet from him, its face threaded with blood, eyes wide and staring, mouth yawning wide, unnaturally so, as if something had been forced in there that dislocated his jaws.

Boyd heard himself begin to sob.

Jurgen's corpse was up there somewhere and Boyd could hear blood dripping earthward like a gentle rain. *Plop, plop, plop.* The light of the lantern illuminated the forest to about twenty feet up and he could see the glistening red drops rolling down the trunk of a petrified seed fern. He was hearing other sounds, too.

The sound of chewing.

And wet sucking sounds.

He felt his mind go. It vacated his brain with nary a scream or a mad peal of laughter. It just went and he was content with that.

He heard her coming down the trunk of a tree with a skittering sound of dozens of legs. She paused on the log that had broken his leg, not five feet away. He could hear her breathing.

But he could not see her.

In that same scraping, metallic squeal of a voice, she said, "*Boooooyyyyyd?*"

He was looking right through her, looking at something that cast no image, something invisible and ancient and lonely. She uttered a cooing sound that made his flesh crawl.

"It's okay," he said, cold sweat running down his face. "I won't hurt you...I won't leave you..."

She moved forward, cooing.

Yes, she was coming for him now.

And he knew she wasn't going to kill him. She had responded to him right from the first and he knew it. He heard her crawl atop Maki's corpse. She smelled ancient and dry, like hay stored in a closed-up barn. Maki's head was lifted up and something stabbed into his throat. There was a sucking, slurping noise.

"Oh no," Boyd whispered under his breath. "Oh Jesus..."

That slurping sound continued and he saw blood...a stream of blood being sucked from Maki's throat with gulping sounds like a thirsty man downing a beer. The stream of blood was sucked into the air, probably into her mouth, then it diffused into several rivulets and filled several kidney-shaped sacs that must have been her stomachs...all three of them.

Boyd watched.

He heard her make smacking sounds as she finished up.

He was shaking and moaning deep in his throat and that wasn't from what he had just seen, but from what she was doing: stroking his arm with something like a spurred finger. And cooing in his ear.

# 18

B oyd opened his eyes.
    It was pitch black.

He did not know how much time had passed. It might have been six days or six months as far as he was concerned, because his mind was lost in a white fog of madness. He was inside one of the cells in the ancient honeycombed trees, a cell near the very top. This is where she had brought him. Where she kept him and cared for him.

His leg had become infected the second day and he submerged into a mire of fever dreams, calling out to people who were not there and remembering a reality that no longer existed for him. The infection would have spread and killed him eventually, but she would not have it. Devoted and kind and heartsick for company, any company, she had tended to him. She had sucked the poison from his leg and cooled him with water she sprayed onto his face.

When he woke from the fever, he screamed.

And she cooed her love for him.

He lay there, trying to remember the world before the cell, but it was all becoming rapidly grainy and indistinct. A dream-world, a pleasant fantasy slipping from his grasp. The lanterns and flashlights were gone, but no matter, their batteries would have been long exhausted by now.

The darkness was forever.

But he was never alone in it.

He recalled when she had first come for him, how she had been almost shy. She had sat at his feet for some time, cooing and clicking, sometimes making a low and haunting musical sort of piping. But he had held out his hand and she had come, hungry for companionship, shattered by an eternity of ungodly isolation. It had not been easy at first getting used to her, the feel of her touch or the squeal of her voice. All those clicking, spidery limbs like tangled, knotty bamboo, the bony rungs of her body that were set with spiny hairs. Her fetid breath, the stink of age and corruption, a sickly warm miasma flavored by what she had been eating.

He did not know what she was.

She was not a spider exactly, but maybe something like one. Something with a convoluted, glossy exoskeleton and countless whispering stick-like limbs. Her flesh felt oily and damp like wet seal skin. But she was no insect or arachnid. She had a head. A long, narrow head and something like a face. A head draped with a mop of greasy, webby hair that undulated like worms when you touched it and a face set with no less than three oval mouths. Sometimes, she would lie next to him and lick him with her tongues, cleaning him and keeping him healthy.

At first, he'd wanted to scream, but even that had passed. He even got used to the food she chewed for him into a fine, moist pulp and regurgitated into his mouth. He did not like to think of what the food was, being that there was only one possible source of meat in the cavern.

It took some getting used to, just as it took getting used to the way she called his name, that rusty, scraping wail that was like the agonized mewling of a cat wailing in the dead of night. "Boooooyyyd," she would shriek with that pathetic childlike screech that was so lonely, so destitute like the squall of a terrified child. "Booooooyyyyd…."

Yes, he had even gotten used to that.

It was amazing what you could get used to, given time.

He could not know what she was or what her race had been. Only that she had known a terrible, wasting loneliness that ripped open her mind. She had waited in stark, hopeless, solitary desertion as her kind had died out. As the continents shifted and the great saurians gave way to the megafauna, as the great Permian age was devastated by mass extinction and the Mesozoic seas became deserts, as mammals claimed the land and men learned to walk and then run, filling the lands above like racing white ants.

How many days?

How many fucking days had it been?

He had read somewhere once that the average human mind will crack after three or four days of absolute darkness. The lack of sensory stimulation makes the mind turn back upon itself and submerge. Boyd could not be sure if he was insane or not. All he could do was wait in the cell. Wait for her to return because she always did.

Listen.

Yes, he heard her. She was coming. *Ticka-ticka-ticka.* She entered the cell and squatted at his feet. He had not seen her for many hours, maybe days. She smelled different. That's how he learned to judge her moods, by the smell she extruded. Today it was very sweet like the odor of cherries. He had never smelled that before. When she was scared it was an odor like dry straw. When she was angry it the smell of pale green bogs. But this…this was new.

He spoke to her but she did not respond.

She waited there at his feet.

It seemed to go on for many hours.

When Boyd opened his eyes again, she was still there. She was making a high singing noise and just beneath it, something else: a fleshy, moist sort of sound like ripe juicy tomatoes were sliding out of her.

And the smell…black, diseased, horrid.

That's when he knew. That's when he understood.

That's when it all began to make a curious and revolting sort of sense.

As she had hibernated through countless ages, a flat dormancy had brooded within her. She had carried a secret from the Permian, she had carried the seed of her kind which waited within her, gestating through the eons.

She was a female.

It was only natural that she give birth.

When it was done and he was whimpering under his breath, she sidled up next to him.

She wanted him to touch her.

At first, Boyd was offended as he felt them clustering on her back, squirming and writhing, but soon he learned to accept. And as they accepted him and ran over him like tiny, mewling rodents, he actually knew he would come to care for them. They flooded over him in a swarm of leggy young, nipping and licking at him. Down there in the dank subterranean blackness, he could remember that once he had been married to a woman named Linda and that she had carried his child.

He had been a father once.

And now he was a father again.

A father with hundreds of children that crawled and skittered and nipped.

He was a lot of things, but he certainly was not lonely.

But as the hours passed, he knew she was growing edgy, tense. She was feeling threatened and he smelled it on her. And sometime later, he knew why: the rumbling. The rock-crushing rumble of a drill. They were digging him out. They were coming to get him.

*Oh no*, he thought. *Don't do that.*

*You don't understand.*

*She's very jealous…*

# 19

It took them a week to open the spider hole back up and three more days to clear out the stope leading to the cavern that Jurgens had told them about over the radio. It was hard going every step of the way, but as the nation held its breath and CNN and NBC camped out at the Hobart Mine and the families waited patiently, they made it to the cavern.

The only thing separating it from them was a wall of rock.

Sonar readings told them it was some five feet deep. They could go through it in a matter of hours.

"Get that drill down here," Russo told them, looking about ten years older than he had when this whole business began. "I want a bore hole into that cavern."

It took about an hour to punch a hole through the rock.

A dry, sucking blast of air blew out at them.

They tried calling out to the men through the pilot hole but got nothing. Thermal imaging cameras were brought in and everyone cheered when they picked up living signatures on the other side.

"Bring in that reamer," Russo said. "Let's open this mother up."

As the crew got to work, Corey aimed a lightweight parabolic microphone into the pilot hole. He handed the headphones to Russo.

"Do you hear it?" Corey said.

"Yes," Russo said. "Yes…"

Somebody was trying to communicate with them.

There was no mistaking the sound from inside the cavern: Click, click, click…

# About the Author

Tim Curran is the author of the novels Skin Medicine, Hive, Dead Sea, Resurrection, Hag Night, Skull Moon, The Devil Next Door, Doll Face, Afterburn, House of Skin, and Biohazard. His short stories have been collected in Bone Marrow Stew and Zombie Pulp. His novellas include The Underdwelling, The Corpse King, Puppet Graveyard, Worm, and Blackout. His short stories have appeared in such magazines as City Slab, Flesh&Blood, Book of Dark Wisdom, and Inhuman, as well as anthologies such as Shadows Over Main Street, Eulogies III, and October Dreams II. His fiction has been translated into German, Japanese, Spanish, and Italian. Find him on Facebook at: https://www.facebook.com/tim.curran.77

## Bibliography

### Novels

*Afterburn*
*Biohazard*
*Cannibal Corpse*
*Dead Sea*
*Doll Face*
*Graveworm*
*Grim Riders*
*Grimweave*
*Hag Night*
*Hive*
*Hive 2: The Spawning*
*House of Skin*
*Long Black Coffin*
*Monstrosity*
*Nightcrawlers*
*Resurrection*
*Skin Medicine*
*Skull Moon*
*Terror Cell*
*The Devil Next Door*

## Novellas

*Blackout*
*Corpse Rider*
*Deadlock*
*Fear Me*
*Headhunter*
*Leviathan*
*Puppet Graveyard*
*Sow*
*Tenebris*
*The Corpse King*
*The Underdwelling*
*Toxic Shadows*
*Worm*

*Collections*

*Bone Marrow Stew*
*Here There be Monsters*
*Zombie Pulp*

Curious about other Crossroad Press books?
Stop by our site:
https://www.crossroadpress.com
We offer quality writing
in digital, audio, and print formats.